UNDERCOVER STUD GAY DETECTIVE

UNDERCOVER STUD GAY DETECTIVE

A DETECTIVE LANCE FORTUNATO GAY MURDER MYSTERY

GRIFF HOLLAND

Paperback ISBN: 9798864869796

Cover Design by Etienne St. Aubert

Book Design by Luca Holland

❀ Created with Vellum

CONTENTS

CHAPTER 1
THE ASSIGNMENT

Detective Lance Fortunato is a charismatic, openly gay police detective known for his sharp instincts and unwavering determination. He is assigned to infiltrate a crime ring that preys on vulnerable individuals within the LGBTQ+ community. To gather evidence against the ring's leaders, Fortunato partners with Officer Jake McDermott, a ruggedly handsome, straight beat cop. Together, they form an unlikely yet compelling duo as they assume new identities and prepare to go undercover in Boston's underground gay scene.

Fortunato is a muscular and attractive man whose presence commands attention, drawing eyes and turning heads wherever he goes. His body, sculpted through years in the gym, accentuates his raw masculinity. Dressed in a perfectly tailored suit that fits him impeccably, he exudes an air of confidence and power that is impossible to ignore. As an out gay man, he embodies the archetype of a "man's man," with a ripped, hairy physique that appeals to more men than he could ever hope to engage.

However, it is Fortunato's eyes that truly captivate those who meet him. They are the color of smoky topaz, sparkling with a depth that seems to draw people in. When Fortunato locks eyes with someone, it feels as if he can see into their very core, unraveling their deepest desires and revealing their vulnerabilities.

Men and women alike find themselves under his spell. Something about him transcends conventional definitions of sexuality, an irresistible force that appeals to the fundamental human desire for strength and power. His sharp instincts and relentless determination only enhance his allure, making it clear that Fortunato is a man who knows what he wants and will stop at nothing to achieve it.

FORTUNATO'S SURROUNDINGS ARE MYSTERIOUS, and his aura of danger thrills and intimidates. This allure draws people in, even as it warns them to approach with caution. He has witnessed and experienced things that most can only imagine, and this knowledge is reflected in his demeanor, which exudes a quiet confidence that seems to radiate from every pore.

Yet beneath this enigmatic exterior lies a vulnerability—a flicker of something deeper. This vulnerability hints at the passion smoldering within him, guarded yet palpable. Those fortunate enough to glimpse this side of Fortunato feel an irresistible urge to peel back the layers and uncover the man behind the badge.

And so, wherever Fortunato went, he left behind a trail of longing glances and whispered conversations. He became the subject of fantasies and daydreams, embodying desire and untamed sensuality. People couldn't help but wonder what lay beneath his calm exterior, what secrets he held, and what passions burned within his soul.

Lance Fortunato was a man of intense allure—a force of nature who captivated all who crossed his path. Whether it was the confident set of his jaw, the way his tailored suit clung to his muscular frame, or the mysterious gleam in his smoky topaz eyes, there was no denying his intoxicating and irresistible power. As he prepared to embark on his latest assignment, delving into the dangerous and seductive world of Boston's underground gay scene, the true depths of Fortunato's allure would be put to the test in a world where desire and danger intertwined in unimaginable ways.

⊏⊐

FORTUNATO STOOD at his chief's desk, protesting. "Geez, boss. A rookie? He's just a boy. And, goddammit, he's straight. Come on, chief. You know this kind of work should be in the hands of experienced gay cops," Fortunato argued.

Chief Hannity tried to calm his best detective. "Fortunato, take a deep breath. McDermott's good, and with your help, he'll make a name for himself on the force. I tried to find a handsome, appealing junior beat cop for you—someone who could pass as gay and connect with the gay crowd."

"Appeal to the gay crowd? What the fuck, chief. Do you think I appeal to the gay crowd? With all due respect, sir, I..."

At that moment, the chief interrupted. "Well, look what the cat dragged in. Good morning, Officer McDermott. Officer Jake McDermott, meet Detective Lance Fortunato," he introduced the officer who had just entered.

⊏⊐

THE YOUNG BEAT cop removed his officer cap and extended his muscular arm to greet Fortunato. "It's a pleasure, sir.

Your reputation on the force is impeccable. I'm really looking forward to working with you."

Fortunato assessed the officer before him: an incredibly handsome, 6-foot-tall blond stud whose muscular physique strained against his tight uniform. He smiled, knowing that the chief was likely laughing to himself.

"Welcome, officer. We need to review the files, so let's get to it."

"Yes, sir. I'm all yours."

Fortunato caught a glance at his chief, who raised an eyebrow and smiled.

"Fuck you, chief," Fortunato whispered in the chief's direction as he exited the office, hearing Hannity's laughter echo from behind the closed door.

<hr>

WHEN LANCE FORTUNATO, the embodiment of raw masculine allure, teamed up with the ruggedly handsome beat cop Jake McDermott, an electric tension crackled in the air. Their partnership was unlikely, a clash of contrasting desires that sent shockwaves of intrigue through their veins. Damn it. Why did he have to be assigned a straight cop for this case? Fortunato felt frustrated, fearing he would have to babysit McDermott.

As the two men worked side by side at Fortunato's desk, the detective couldn't shake the feeling that McDermott's deep blue eyes were often drawn to him, stealing glances at his body. There was an intensity in that gaze, a hunger that seemed to devour every inch of Fortunato's sculpted physique. He recognized that look, and it thrilled and terrified him.

Fortunato knew he needed to maintain professionalism and keep their interactions strictly business. But the undeniable magnetic pull between them was palpable, an invisible force drawing them closer with each passing moment. Fortunato felt the heat of McDermott's gaze searing into his skin.

Yet, Fortunato was confused. McDermott, who identified as heterosexual, was an enigma to him. He represented a forbidden fruit and a secret longing simmering beneath the surface. The knowledge that McDermott's attractions lay outside societal expectations only intensified their seductive tension.

FORTUNATO AND MCDERMOTT shared an undeniable connection. It was evident in the way their bodies moved in sync and in the lingering promise of their glances. Desire hung in the air between them, a delicate balance of temptation and restraint that threatened to shatter with each stolen glance and accidental touch.

Fortunato's heart raced with each encounter, each moment of unexpected connection. He yearned to explore the depths of McDermott's desires and unravel the hidden secrets within him. However, he was acutely aware of the risks involved and the potential consequences that could jeopardize their partnership and expose their forbidden yearning to the world.

Yet the fire burning within Fortunato could not be extinguished. It consumed him, driving him to push the boundaries of their connection and test the limits of their desires. He craved the taste of McDermott's lips and the touch of his strong hands on his body. A hunger drove him to the edge of reason, a longing that demanded to be fulfilled.

In the swirling vortex of their unlikely partnership, Fortunato and McDermott grappled with the undeniable chemistry simmering beneath the surface. It was a dance of temptation and restraint, a game of risk and reward. As they ventured into

Boston's underground gay scene, they discovered that the line between professionalism and passion was blurrier than they had ever imagined.

———

FORTUNATO WAS FRUSTRATED at the thought of spending time with this straight guy, trying to teach him how to pass as gay. The guy screamed "heterosexual" and would stand out like a cop in any covert operation. Great.

"Looks like it's your day, McDermott. You and I are hitting the gay bars tonight, and you're going to do your best to blend in as a gay man. You'll watch, listen, and absorb everything you can about gay culture so you can fit in—and so you don't put my life in jeopardy. Do we have an understanding?"

"Yes, sir," McDermott replied, a hint of eagerness in his voice. "You want me to seamlessly blend in as a gay man, making sure no one suspects my true intentions while we're undercover."

Fortunato smirked, mischief dancing in his eyes. "Exactly, my man. We need to be convincing, and I believe you're up for the challenge."

McDermott's heart raced with excitement as he nodded in agreement. "With your expert guidance, I'm confident I'll quickly learn how to assimilate."

———

FORTUNATO LEANED IN CLOSER, his voice dropping to a low, seductive tone. "My guidance, huh? Do you think I give off the aura of a gay man, McDermott?" He paused, a playful smirk tugging at his lips. "Never mind that. We're leaving this place behind. You'll be staying at my condo for our undercover assignment. Understand?"

Heat surged through McDermott's veins, his pulse quickening at the thought of sharing close living quarters with Fortunato. "Yes, sir," he replied, his voice barely above a whisper. "Thank you, sir. Should I go home to pack a bag?"

Fortunato's eyes sparkled with mischief as he waved away the idea. "No need, McDermott. It seems we have more in common than just this mission. I believe we're the same size. You'll wear my clothes to enhance our image as a gay couple." He playfully punched McDermott's arm, a flicker of desire passing between them. "Grab the stack of files, and let's head to my place. We'll change there, and I'll show you how to embrace this role in public fully."

As they exited the room, anticipation crackled in the air, propelling them forward. McDermott couldn't help but wonder what secrets Fortunato would reveal in the intimacy of his condo and how deeply they would delve into their undercover personas.

————

THE TWO STRIKING men arrived at Fortunato's luxurious third-story condo in Dorchester, where the atmosphere was thick with a potent blend of desire and anticipation. McDermott admired the space, scanning the tasteful decor and the subtle hints of sensuality that infused every corner.

"Nice place, sir," McDermott remarked, his voice revealing a note of admiration.

"Thanks, dude," Fortunato replied, a smoldering glint in his eyes. "Set the files down on the table. We'll come back to them later. For now, let's shake off the pressure and relax a bit."

Fortunato's bedroom beckoned, and the two men moved in its direction. "Okay, strip down, dude," Fortunato commanded, his voice dripping with seductive authority. "You can hang your uniform in the closet. I'll find something suitable for you to wear."

McDermott's heart raced with a mix of nervousness and excitement. He hesitated momentarily, locking eyes with Fortunato before summoning the courage to undress in front of another man, especially one as striking as Fortunato. With a deep breath, he began to undress, each garment falling away to reveal his toned physique beneath.

⬛▭

HIS SHIRT and T-shirt were discarded, followed by his belt and pants. Fortunato's gaze lingered appreciatively, tracing the contours of McDermott's body with an intensity that quickened his pulse. 'Shit,' he thought. 'This dude is ripped as hell.'

Fortunato pointed to a drawer where McDermott could securely store his gun and ammunition, serving as a silent reminder that they were shedding not only their uniforms but also the weight of their respective roles.

Standing before Fortunato in his boxer shorts, McDermott felt utterly vulnerable. A surge of desire coursed through Fortunato; a primal hunger mirrored McDermott's yearning. Fortunato, too, succumbed to the moment's pull, shedding his suit, shirt, and T-shirt with deliberate movements, revealing his sculpted physique that left McDermott breathless. 'I'm straight. I'm straight,' McDermott kept repeating to himself. 'What the hell is going on here? This man is amazing.'

In the dimly lit room, Fortunato stood before McDermott in nothing but a pair of low-rise Calvin briefs, the fabric clinging to his form perfectly. The detective's pouch was obscenely large and stretched to the max. Tension filled the room as their eyes locked, a silent agreement passing between them—this was the beginning of something extraordinary.

THE BOUNDARIES that had defined them melted away, leaving only two men stripped down to their most authentic selves, exposing their vulnerabilities and ready to explore the depths of pleasure ahead.

In that softly lit room, McDermott was confused. A stage was set, and his body was at odds with his mind. His eyes hungrily roamed over Fortunato's sculpted physique, the enticing contours and curves calling to him with irresistible allure.

"First lesson, McDermott," Fortunato purred, his voice a sultry melody that resonated deep within McDermott's core. "For gay men, underwear is meant to showcase your assets, to tantalize and entice, not to hide them like those boxer shorts. After all, we're both men who appreciate the beauty of our bodies, right? You've worked hard in the gym. Look at you—you're a fucking stud in old man underwear," Fortunato chuckled, eliciting a smile from McDermott.

Desire coursed through McDermott, mixing nervousness with excitement. "Yes, sir," he replied, his voice revealing a hunger he could no longer suppress. "But if you don't mind my asking, how big is your cock?"

FORTUNATO LAUGHED HEARTILY. Closing the distance between them, he reached out to tousle McDermott's blond curls, his touch sending electric shivers down McDermott's spine. "Ah, my eager student," he said, a glint of mischief in his eyes. "Finally, a truly gay question. You're learning quickly, my boy. Well, let's just say I possess a solid twelve inches when fully engorged. And what about you?"

McDermott's eyes widened, his breath catching in his throat. "Fuck," he whispered, his voice trembling with admiration. "Twelve inches... I've only dared to dream about a man like you, sir. I've got nine inches, sir."

Fortunato's gaze intensified, a smoldering fire igniting in his eyes. "Nine inches? There's no shame in that, boy. Most men would kill to be with someone like you."

"Really, Fortunato?"

"Really, dude. You're hung like a stallion. You have nothing to worry about in the cock department, my man."

McDermott blushed, pleased to receive a compliment from the stud of a detective.

THE TWO MEN STOOD CLOSE, clearly checking each other out. They both knew what they wanted but hesitated to cross the line. Fortunato caught McDermott's gaze and held it. Then, unexpectedly, McDermott's eyes began to water, and he felt tears fall.

Fortunato immediately wrapped his arms around him, holding him tight. He closed the distance between them, an irresistible magnetism drawing them together. With a touch as gentle as a whisper, he caressed McDermott's cheek, his thumb tracing a tantalizing path along his lower lip. "It's okay, stud. You're with me. I won't hurt you; I promise," he murmured, his voice seductive and comforting.

McDermott's pulse quickened, and his senses heightened as he surrendered himself to Fortunato.

"I'm sorry, detective," Officer Jake McDermott said, his voice filled with regret. "I don't know how this happened. I've always been straight. Always. I guess I was just overwhelmed by the situation. You're so attractive, Fortunato, and I've found myself drawn to you. Being alone in my room, just wearing my underwear, feels exhilarating. You have an incredible body—those muscles, that perfect ass. Everything about you is stunning. I just don't know what to do, sir."

⸻

"I UNDERSTAND, McDermott. You can trust me completely," Fortunato said softly, his voice comforting and dispelling any doubts. McDermott's heart raced with anticipation and vulnerability.

"What's happening, detective?" he managed to ask, curiosity tinged with apprehension.

"We're embarking on a journey, McDermott," Fortunato replied, his tone filled with compassion. "A journey of connection and discovery. Just surrender to the moment, let go of any resistance, and allow yourself to be enveloped by the energy around you. Give yourself permission to experience every sensation, every touch."

"Permission? Permission for what, exactly, sir?" McDermott asked, his voice trembling with a mix of intrigue and desire.

"Permission to explore, McDermott," Fortunato replied, his voice a velvety whisper. "Permission to delve into pleasure, to uncover your desires. To unleash your capacity to feel and express passion. To define our connection."

CHAPTER 2
COP AND DETECTIVE SEX

The weight of Det. Lance Fortunato's words descended upon Officer Jake McDermott's senses, their gravity igniting a firestorm within his mind. Uncertainty and anticipation mingled, creating a heady cocktail that coursed through his veins. McDermott's voice quivered as he dared to voice the unspoken question between them, his words dripping with longing.

"Sir, are you suggesting...?" McDermott began, his voice a delicate tremor, his breath catching in his throat.

"Yes, McDermott," Fortunato affirmed, his voice a sultry caress that resonated with undeniable truth. "I want you. I've hungered for you since our eyes locked when the currents of desire surged between us. I want you, McDermott."

⊏⊐

MCDERMOTT'S BREATH HITCHED, his pulse quickening as the raw honesty in Fortunato's voice carved deep grooves of anticipation within him. The whirlwind of emotions threatened to consume him, and he sought reassurance in Fortunato's gaze, his voice a thread of hope.

"Sir, can I trust what you're saying?" McDermott questioned, his voice a plea for certainty amidst the tempest of their desires.

"Feel it, McDermott," Fortunato urged, his voice a seductive melody, weaving its enchantment around McDermott's senses. "Feel the undeniable chemistry that crackles between us, an electric symphony of passion. Believe in us."

McDermott's body trembled, every nerve ablaze with a newfound intensity. The energy that sparked between them was a symphony of desire, a force that defied description. McDermott's voice, barely more than a whisper, carried the weight of awe and desire.

"Fuck, yes, sir," he confessed, his voice a reverent murmur laden with wonder. "The energy that binds us is fucking indescribable, a fusion of longing and lust that sets my soul ablaze."

⊏━━⊐

"TRUST YOURSELF, MCDERMOTT," Fortunato breathed, his voice a gentle caress that soothed McDermott's uncertainties. "Trust in the moment, the electric current that brings us together. Your instincts will guide you if you allow them to. Let go of your inhibitions and surrender."

McDermott's eyes searched Fortunato's face, a mixture of longing and trepidation reflected in his gaze. "Detective, are you certain about this? I've never engaged in gay sex before. I've never even jerked off with another guy. I've always believed I was straight."

Fortunato's touch was firm and tender as he cupped McDermott's cheek, his thumb gently stroking the smooth skin.

"McDermott, listen to my words," he whispered, his voice a velvet promise. "Stop overthinking, and let yourself feel. Your body knows what it craves, what ignites your deepest passions. Listen to the rhythm of your heart, the primal beat that pulses through your veins. Can you do that for me, McDermott?"

A flicker of determination sparked in McDermott's eyes as he nodded, his breath catching in his throat. "I think so, sir," he replied, his voice laced with a newfound resolve. "Yes, sir. I can try. Thank you, sir."

FORTUNATO'S SMILE was both encouraging and full of promise. "Good man," he murmured, his voice brimming with satisfaction. "Now, get rid of those ridiculous boxer shorts. They are concealing the best part of your body, dude."

"Yes, sir," McDermott responded with anticipation and vulnerability. His fingers trembled slightly as he reached for the waistband of his boxers, slowly pulling them down revealing his naked form to Fortunato's hungry gaze. The cool air embraced his exposed skin, heightening his awareness of every inch of his body.

Fortunato's eyes drank in the sight before him, his gaze a smoldering fire that ignited McDermott's desire. "You are magnificent, McDermott," he breathed, his voice husky with desire. "Every curve, every line of your body is a work of art. And now, my dear McDermott, it's time to explore this masterpiece together."

McDermott's heart raced as Fortunato closed the distance between them, their bodies mere inches apart. The air crackled with an intoxicating tension, a magnetic pull that drew them closer. Their lips met in a searing kiss, a collision of passion and hunger, as their bodies melded together in a dance of desire.

"THAT'S IT, MCDERMOTT," Fortunato's voice resonated with admiration and desire, his eyes devouring McDermott's transformed physique. "Damn, dude. You're beyond incredible. Your body is a masterpiece."

McDermott's chest heaved with pride, his newfound confidence radiating from every sculpted muscle. "Thank you, sir," he replied, his voice laced with a hint of awe. "But compared to you, Fortunato, I pale in comparison. You're like a Greek god, a vision of masculine perfection."

Fortunato's grin was both playful and alluring. "Aw, thanks, McDermott," he murmured, his voice a velvet caress. "But this moment is about you. Show me your cock, McDermott. Let me feast my eyes upon it." His tone dripped with anticipation, a hunger that mirrored McDermott's own.

The air thickened as McDermott lifted his heavy cock, opening his hand for Fortunato to see his engorged manhood. Fortunato's gaze intensified, fixated on the sight before him. "Wow, McDermott," he breathed, his voice husky with desire. "Nine inches. Impressive. Very impressive indeed. I need that cock, dude."

McDermott's hand trembled slightly as he wrapped his fingers around his pulsating length, the touch sending a jolt of pleasure through his entire being. "Like this, sir?" he asked, his voice thick with need. "Should I stroke it?"

FORTUNATO'S EYES never left McDermott's hand, his arousal evident as he watched the tempting display. "Yes, McDermott," he whispered, his voice filled with raw desire. "Stroke it. Slowly. Let your hand glide up and down, feeling the surge of blood rushing into it, making it harder, more alive. Embrace the sensations, McDermott. Let them guide you."

As McDermott obeyed, his hand moved with rhythmic precision, pleasure mingling with the tension in the room. "God, this feels insane," he muttered, his voice a blend of disbelief and ecstasy.

Fortunato leaned closer, his breath hot against McDermott's ear. "It is, dude," he admitted, his voice a low, seductive murmur. "But don't stop. Keep going. Keep exploring. Feel the pleasure building inside you, like a wildfire consuming your senses. Don't fight it, McDermott. Surrender to it. Let it wash over you, wave after wave. You're doing amazing, McDermott."

McDermott's grip tightened, his strokes becoming more fervent as the pleasure intensified. The world around him faded into a blur of sensation; his focus centered solely on the pleasure coursing through his veins. He surrendered to the moment, allowing himself to be consumed by the intoxicating dance of pleasure and desire.

⊏⊐

"FORTUNATO," McDermott's voice quivered with disbelief and unbridled desire, his body alive with sensations he couldn't ignore. "This is crazy. I don't understand why, but this intense arousal drives me insane. Would you... would you mind taking off your briefs for me, sir?"

A knowing smile tugged at the corners of Fortunato's lips as he met McDermott's gaze, his eyes filled with a smoldering heat. "Of course, McDermott," he purred, his voice dripping with seduction. "Watch closely."

As Fortunato discarded the last barrier between them, revealing his magnificent manhood, McDermott's breath hitched in his throat. "Holy shit, dude," he gasped, his voice laced with awe. "Twelve inches? That's fucking massive. I can't believe it. Holy shit."

Fortunato's grin grew wider, basking in the appreciation that emanated from McDermott's gaze. "Do you like what you see, McDermott?" he inquired.

"Like it, sir?" McDermott's eyes widened, his voice tinged with excitement and reverence. "I'm obsessed, Fortunato. You are masculine perfection."

McDermott and Fortunato stood naked before each other, their bodies sharing vulnerability and desire. McDermott's voice trembled softly, his words barely a whisper. "This feels incredible, sir, being this exposed with you."

———

FORTUNATO'S VOICE was low and commanding, "Yes, McDermott," he murmured. "We're stripped bare, physically and emotionally. We've built a trust. Now, embrace your desire. McDermott, stroke your cock for me. Do it for me, stud."

McDermott's hand trembled as he wrapped his fingers around his pulsating length, his eyes never leaving Fortunato's gaze. With each stroke, he felt pleasure, sensations that threatened to overwhelm him. "Okay, sir," he breathed, his voice laced with longing.

Encouragement flowed from Fortunato's lips as McDermott surrendered to his pleasure. "That's it, McDermott," he encouraged, his voice a seductive murmur. "You're a natural. Keep stroking. Up and down. It feels good, doesn't it, McDermott?"

McDermott's breaths grew ragged, his grip tightening as the pleasure intensified. "Oh, yeah," he moaned, his voice laced with need. "Yeah. It feels so fucking good, sir. I'm losing myself stroking in front of you."

———

"DON'T HOLD BACK, MCDERMOTT," Fortunato's voice resonated with encouragement and a hint of command. "Explore every sensation, indulge your curiosities, and find what truly ignites your desire. Let yourself be carried away by the waves of pleasure. You're doing phenomenal, bud."

McDermott's breath hitched as his body responded to the intoxicating journey of self-discovery. "God, this is beyond incredible," he gasped, his voice thick with need. "It's the hottest, most mindblowing experience I've ever had. I'm so hard, Fortunato. So fucking hard."

Fortunato's low and seductive voice fueled the fire that consumed them both. "Yes, dude," he murmured, his words a sultry invitation. "Now, reach out and take hold of my cock. Grip it as if it were your own. Explore its length, its girth. Feel its weight in your hand."

McDermott's fingers trembled with anticipation as they wrapped around Fortunato's throbbing member. "Wow," he breathed, his voice filled with awe. "It's so fucking thick and heavy, sir. Every inch of it is a testament to masculine perfection."

<hr />

"STROKE IT, MCDERMOTT," Fortunato commanded, his voice a potent mix of authority and desire. "Wrap those strong fingers around it and stroke. Explore the rhythm that brings us both pleasure. Yes, that's it. Good boy. Let your touch guide you."

As McDermott complied, his strokes grew more confident, his grip tightening with each movement. Pleasure surged through him, mingling with the arousal that enveloped the room. "What do you think, McDermott?" Fortunato's voice dripped with anticipation. "Is it everything you've dreamed about?"

McDermott's voice trembled with a mix of vulnerability and raw desire. "More, sir," he confessed, his breaths ragged. "It's way more than I've ever imagined. The intensity, the connection we share... it's beyond my wildest dreams."

Fortunato's voice, filled with reassurance, cut through McDermott's doubts. "No, McDermott," he assured, his tone firm yet gentle. "There's nothing wrong with you. We're simply two men embracing our desires, and our bodies respond accordingly. Look, your cock is leaking pre-cum. It's a natural response to the pleasure we're experiencing."

McDermott's eyes widened, a mix of surprise and concern. "Is that normal, sir?" he asked, his voice tinged with uncertainty.

▭▭

FORTUNATO'S VOICE held a soothing warmth as he replied, "Absolutely, dude. The more aroused and excited we become, the more pre-cum will leak from our cocks. It's a sign that we're fully immersed in the pleasure we share. There's no reason to feel ashamed or embarrassed."

McDermott's body relaxed as he absorbed Fortunato's reassurance. "Okay, sir," he whispered, his voice filled with trust. "If you say so, sir. I'll relax."

"Trust me, dude. Now, let's keep stroking. Feel the pleasure building inside you. Get a little faster. Yep, that's it. Keep going. Don't stop. Let the sensations take over."

"I'm so close, sir," McDermott gasped, his voice heavy with urgency. "Oh, fuck. I'm on the edge, teetering right there."

Fortunato's desire surged, mirroring McDermott's. "Me too, buddy," he breathed, his voice laced with need. "Come closer, McDermott. Put your cock next to mine and feel the heat and connection. I want us to explode together, dude."

MCDERMOTT OBEYED, shifting his body, their hardened members now pressed against each other. The sensation electrified them both, intensifying the already overwhelming pleasure. "Yes, sir," McDermott moaned, his voice strained. "Oh, god. This is insane. The way our bodies fit together, the way it feels... It's so fucking great."

Fortunato's voice dripped with anticipation, his words a seductive promise. "I love this, McDermott," he murmured, his voice low and husky. "I'm going to pump my load out onto your hot cock. I want to give you everything I can."

McDermott's breath hitched, his body trembling with the impending release. "Oh, fuck," he whimpered, his voice a desperate plea. "Oh, fuck. I'm on the edge, sir. I'm going to shoot. I can't hold it back."

Fortunato's voice, filled with an intoxicating mix of command and encouragement, pushed McDermott further toward the edge. "Do it, McDermott," he growled, his voice a primal invitation. "Shoot that huge load for me, stud. Do it for me, dude. Cum, dude. Cum!"

The dam of restraint shattered as McDermott's body convulsed with ecstasy. "Oh, god!" he cried, his voice echoing through the room. "Oh, god! Oh, god! Ahhh! Ahhh! Ahhh! Yes! Yes! Yes! It feels so fucking good! So fucking good!"

Fortunato's pleasure mingled with McDermott's, their climaxes converging in a release. "Yeah, buddy!" he roared, his voice filled with triumph and delight. "Shoot that massive load. Feel it surge through you, pulsating with pleasure. Let go, dude. Let it all out."

MCDERMOTT'S BODY continued to tremble, his breaths ragged as the intensity of the orgasm washed over him. "Ahhh! Ahhh! Ahhh!" he moaned, his voice a testament to the intensity of their connection. "Geez, that was... that was intense, Fortunato."

Fortunato chuckled, his voice filled with satisfaction. "You're telling me, dude," he replied, his tone still laced with desire. "What a massive load you unloaded. Damn, you're a mess."

A playful smirk tugged at McDermott's lips. "So are you, Fortunato."

Fortunato's eyes sparkled with mischief and affection. "Well, then," he said, his voice filled with warmth, "come here, buddy. Let's clean each other up."

A smile spread across McDermott's face, his desire reignited by the invitation. "Thanks, man," he murmured, his voice laced with appreciation. "That's incredibly hot."

⊏⊐

THE STEAM-FILLED bathroom enveloped McDermott and Fortunato as they stepped into the spacious shower, the glass enclosure offering a glimpse of their naked, glistening bodies. Soft, warm droplets of water cascaded from the showerhead above, creating a sensual mist that clung to their heated skin.

The tiled walls, adorned with intricate patterns, provided a backdrop of understated elegance. The cool, smooth surface offered a contrasting touch against their flushed bodies, amplifying the sensuality of their encounter.

The shower itself was generously sized, allowing them ample room to move and explore. The sleek fixtures, gleaming with polished chrome, exuded a modern sophistication that complemented the raw masculinity of the two men.

As the steam swirled around them, their shadows danced in the ethereal haze, their silhouettes merging and separating like a passionate embrace frozen in time. The warm water flowed over their bodies, caressing their skin and accentuating the curves and contours that defined them as men.

The scent of shower gel filled the air, mingling with the musky aroma of their arousal. The steam carried their heated breaths, creating an intimate atmosphere that seemed to heighten their connection, drawing them closer together.

⸻

AS THEY STOOD beneath the cascading water, their eyes met, gazes filled with desire, trust, and a hunger for more. McDermott's hand reached out, fingers tracing along the smooth surface of the tiles, before finding Fortunato's waist, pulling him closer. Their bodies pressed together, the heat escalating as the water continued to rain down, creating an intimacy of sensations.

The two men kissed passionately, finally bringing love into the connection between the two studs. McDermott was unwilling to let Fortunato go. This was not a game to him. This was not an exercise in going undercover. Fortunato could tell immediately that this was real for McDermott. He was in love. And he was all his.

CHAPTER 3
GAY BAR BLOWJOB

Det. Lance Fortunato's gaze bore into Office Jake McDermott's, a mix of admiration and desire flickering in his eyes. "Nine inches, my eager student, is nothing short of fantastic. There's no shame in that, believe me. Most gay men would give anything to have a nine-inch stud like you in their grasp, craving your touch."

A surge of confidence coursed through McDermott, emboldened by Fortunato's words. His insecurities began to melt away as he absorbed the praise. "Really, sir?" he stammered, a note of disbelief in his voice. "I wouldn't even know where to begin having sex with a man, sir."

Fortunato closed the distance between them, his presence towering and commanding. With a gentle touch, he cupped McDermott's chin, his thumb tracing a tantalizing path along the younger man's jawline. "Fear not, my eager apprentice," he murmured, his voice a velvety caress. "I will guide you, show you the depths of pleasure within the realm of man-to-man connection. We can explore every inch of desire you have together, stud."

McDermott's heart raced, anticipation mingling with a newfound sense of liberation. He surrendered himself to Fortunato's experienced touch, his body aflame with a hunger he hadn't known existed. He told himself he was ready to experience the intoxicating world of gay desire fully.

⊏⊐

MCDERMOTT'S SENSES HEIGHTENED, acutely aware of Fortunato's presence beside him. The air crackled with electricity, charged with unspoken longing.

Fortunato turned to McDermott, his gaze intense, locking their eyes in a silent agreement. The weight of their desires hung between them, mingling with the undeniable attraction simmering beneath the surface.

Their bodies gravitated toward each other as if drawn by an invisible force. McDermott's breath hitched as Fortunato's hand brushed against his, their fingers intertwining in a delicate dance. It was a simple touch, yet it promised something more profound.

Their eyes spoke volumes, silently conveying their shared desire. McDermott's pulse quickened as Fortunato's lips descended upon his, a soft collision of warmth and longing. Time seemed to stand still as their mouths melded together, tongues exploring, igniting a fire that burned deep within them.

Their embrace grew intense as their bodies pressed against each other, exploring the contours and curves that defined them. McDermott reveled in Fortunato's firm yet gentle hands roaming his body, leaving trails of searing heat in their wake.

McDermott's inhibitions melted away with each caress, replaced by a new and fabulous hunger, a craving to explore every inch of Fortunato's hot body.

⸺

IN THE DEPTHS of Boston's underground gay scene, where desire thrived in the shadows, Fortunato and McDermott found themselves trapped in a web of forbidden attraction. Their eyes locked, holding a gaze that lingered with a hunger impossible to ignore. Every accidental brush of their fingertips sent an electric surge coursing through their bodies, igniting a flame that burned with a fervor they couldn't resist.

Fortunato felt his pulse quicken in the presence of McDermott, his heart pounding with a rhythm that matched the thumping bass of the club. The air crackled with anticipation, their connection steeped in a compelling danger. They were undercover agents sworn to uphold the law, but the allure of their mutual desire became irresistible, pulling them closer with each passing moment.

IN THE DEPTHS of Boston's underground gay scene, where desire thrived in the shadows, Fortunato and McDermott found themselves trapped in a web of forbidden attraction. Their eyes locked, holding a gaze that lingered with a hunger impossible to ignore. Every accidental brush of their fingertips sent an electric surge coursing through their bodies, igniting a flame that burned with a fervor they couldn't resist.

Fortunato felt his pulse quicken in the presence of McDermott, his heart pounding with a rhythm that matched the thumping bass of the club. The air crackled with anticipation, their connection steeped in a compelling danger. They were undercover agents sworn to uphold the law, but the allure of their mutual desire became irresistible, pulling them closer with each passing moment.

Fortunato led the rookie cop to a local gay bar to see how the younger man would react. Would he freak out? Could he pass as gay? Could he adopt a gay persona in public? And the best question of all for Fortunato was, would the stud actually enjoy it and get off on the experience? Fortunato hoped for the latter.

The two detectives sat at the bar, ordered drinks, and surveyed the scene. The atmosphere was charged with a palpable energy, the air thick with a heady mix of lust and desire. The magnetic pull between the two men intensified, their bodies inching closer, propelled by an invisible force that defied reason. Their gazes locked, a silent conversation unfolding, their eyes becoming windows to the depths of their shared longing.

⊏───⊐

FORTUNATO'S hungry gaze checked out the rookie's sculpted body, his pulse quickening at the sight of his masculinity. A surge of arousal coursed through him, his cock responding eagerly to the stud before him. Fortunato had handpicked McDermott's attire, selecting a v-neck T-shirt that clung to the contours of his biceps and accentuated the swell of his pecs. The fabric strained against the hardness of his nipples, a compelling display that left nothing to the imagination.

Tight jeans encased McDermott's form, their snugness emphasizing every curve and contour as if sculpted to accentuate his bulging cock. Fortunato had insisted that McDermott forego a belt and leave the top button of his jeans undone, a subtle invitation to explore his hidden treasures. McDermott had acquiesced with a surge of confidence and sensuality surging through his body, rendering him utterly irresistible.

Combining the revealing ensemble and McDermott's self-assured poise created an intoxicating cocktail of erotic energy. He felt a newfound sense of empowerment cloaked in an undeniable sexiness. Every movement, every shift of his body, sent ripples of desire through the air, drawing Fortunato closer.

"YOU LOOK ABSOLUTELY FUCKING IRRESISTIBLE, MCDERMOTT," Fortunato breathed, his voice a low, husky growl laden with a raw desire that sent a surge of heat through McDermott's veins.

"Thank you, sir," the rookie replied, his voice betraying a mix of bashfulness and arousal as a rosy flush adorned his cheeks, accentuating his handsome features.

Unable to resist the magnetic pull between them any longer, Fortunato seized the moment, a primal instinct taking hold. With a possessive growl, he pulled the rookie into his arms, their bodies melding together.

McDermott's heart thumped wildly within his chest, a thunderous rhythm mirroring the intensity of their connection. Fortunato's intoxicating scent, a heady blend of masculinity and desire, enveloped him, igniting a firestorm of sensations that coursed through his every nerve.

"Sir," McDermott whispered, his voice a delicate tremor, his breath hitching with excitement and apprehension. "What are we doing? This is a public bar, sir."

A mischievous glimmer danced in Fortunato's eyes as his lips brushed against the shell of the rookie's ear, his voice a seductive murmur that sent shivers down McDermott's spine. "We're just two men reveling in each other's company, McDermott," Fortunato murmured, his voice laced with a potent blend of authority and reassurance. "Let 'em watch, let 'em wonder. This moment is ours, and it's OK for them to watch the heat between us."

McDermott's protests faded into a hushed silence as Fortunato's skilled hands began exploring, tracing the contours of the rookie's muscular back. The sensation of Fortunato's touch, both tender and possessive, sent waves of pleasure cascading through McDermott's body, erasing any lingering doubts or inhibitions.

In that dimly lit bar amidst the prying eyes of strangers, McDermott surrendered himself to the intoxicating dance of desire. With a nod of acquiescence, he let go of his reservations, allowing himself to be swept away by Fortunato's skilled fingers.

———

"THAT'S IT," Fortunato purred, his lips trailing along the rookie's jawline.

"Oh, God," the rookie gasped, his body responding to the detective's touch. "Your body is so hot, Fortunato. Fuck."

Fortunato's body was masculine perfection, every inch crafted with meticulous attention to detail. His broad shoulders commanded attention, hinting at the strength and power within. The sinewy muscles of his arms rippled with definition, evidence of countless hours spent honing his physique. Veins snaked across his forearms, accentuating their rugged appeal.

His chest was a work of art, a chiseled expanse that invited exploration. Each pectoral muscle stood firm and defined, a testament to his dedication and discipline. The taut plains of his abdomen beckoned, etched with a tantalizing six-pack that begged to be traced with fingertips and explored with hungry lips.

"Just imagine how many guys are wishing they were in my place right now, touching this hot body," Fortunato teased, his hands sliding down the rookie's hips.

"Mmm," the rookie moaned, his cock straining against the tight fabric of his jeans.

"They're all watching us, McDermott," Fortunato murmured, his lips ghosting over the rookie's. "They want you so bad. I bet some of them are even jerking off, imagining what it would be like to fuck you."

⊏⊐

"OH, SHIT," the rookie groaned, a surge of desire pulsating at the mere thought. Fortunato's stirred a primal hunger within him, igniting a fire. With a daring touch, Fortunato's fingers slipped beneath the waistband of the rookie's jeans down into his underwear pouch. The tips of his fingers were soon tracing a path along his heated skin.

A gasp escaped the rookie's lips, his body arching instinctively, seeking more of the electrifying contact. The detective's words danced in his head, reaching deep into the recesses of his mind. The vision of a line of eager men, their desire palpable, waiting their turn to experience the exquisite pleasure of his tight, yearning ass, sent a shiver of anticipation through his veins.

"Yes," the rookie hissed, a mixture of need and surrender, his hips grinding against Fortunato's hand, desperate for more. The intensity in his eyes revealed a hunger that matched the older man's, their desires merging in a dance of raw, unapologetic passion.

A devilish smirk played on Fortunato's lips as his fingers wrapped around the rookie's throbbing shaft, exerting a delicious pressure that made the younger man's breath hitch. The world around them blurred into insignificance as the sensations consumed their senses, leaving only the primal connection between them. Throughout the bar, men had put down their drinks as they watched the hunk of stud giving the younger stallion a handjob inside his jeans.

Moans filled the air as the rookie's control slipped away, replaced by a wild abandon that fueled his every movement. Fortunato's skilled touch guided him to ecstasy, his strokes establishing a rhythm that brought him closer to the edge of pleasure with each passing moment.

⊏⊐

ECSTASY CASCADED through the rookie's body, his mind consumed by an overwhelming tide of pleasure. He was a vessel of desire, a willing participant in this intoxicating dance of lust and longing. The anticipation bore down upon him, his cock aching for release, aching to surrender to his release.

A wicked grin played on Fortunato's lips as he whispered words that ignited a primal hunger within the rookie. "Let's give these hungry customers a show, my stud," he murmured, his voice laced with desire and command.

The rookie's breath caught in his throat as he nodded, his hips meeting Fortunato's grip with urgency.

"Come on, McDermott," Fortunato urged, his hand pumping the rookie's cock furiously. "Show them how much you love getting off in front of a crowd. Show them how much you love being a dirty little slut."

"Ahh," the rookie cried, his body tensing as his orgasm crashed over him.

As their bodies slowly stilled, the rookie basked in the afterglow, his chest rising and falling with each ragged breath. The air was heavy with the scent of their shared passion.

"That's it, come for me, McDermott," Fortunato demanded, his grip milking the rookie's pulsing cock.

"Fuck," the rookie groaned, his hips jerking erratically as his release spurted from his cock into his underwear.

"So fucking hot," Fortunato murmured, his gaze drinking in the sight of the spent, panting rookie.

"Jesus," the rookie breathed, his chest heaving as his body recovered.

"You're a natural kid," Fortunato grinned, his fingers swiping the cum dripping down the younger man's thighs.

"Fuck, sir," the rookie sighed, his body relaxing into the older man's embrace.

"Feels good, doesn't it?"

"Yeah," the rookie agreed, his eyes meeting the detectives.

⊂⊃

MCDERMOTT LOOKED AT FORTUNATO, who winked at him. The two men quickly stripped off their tight T-shirts, jeans, and sexy underwear. McDermott was glad to rid himself of his cum-soaked briefs.

MCDERMOTT'S HUNGER for more action surged through him like an unstoppable force, his primal desires awakening under the guise of his undercover persona. A mischievous grin tugged at his lips as he marveled at the seamless transformation from a straight cop to a seductive, insatiable gay man. The lines between reality and fantasy blurred, and he embraced the intoxicating thrill of this clandestine game.

"Damn, you're a natural at this, McDermott. For an undercover straight cop, you sure know how to play the role of a horny gay man," Fortunato whispered huskily, his voice laced with admiration and desire. The heat between them simmered, a tantalizing current that pulsed through the air, igniting the flames of their shared passion.

McDermott's gaze locked with Fortunato's, their eyes speaking volumes in the silent language of desire. "Maybe it's because of my inspiration, Fortunato."

A jolt of excitement coursed through him as the bartender rang the bell, a siren call that heralded a moment of uninhibited sensuality. The air buzzed with anticipation as half-price drink specials were announced. Just as he said that, the bartender rang the bell, announcing that it was time for half-price drink specials for men who stripped entirely down for the rest of the evening.

Bags were distributed among the eager crowd, their contents destined to embrace the clothing that would soon be shed, casting away the restraints of modesty. A wave of exhilaration washed over McDermott as he realized everyone was seizing this opportunity, embracing their carnal desires without hesitation.

IN A SWIFT MOTION, McDermott's gaze met Fortunato's, a silent agreement that echoed through their souls. The fabric that had concealed their sculpted forms fell away, leaving them vulnerable and exposed, their bodies bared to the world with an audacious confidence. The tight T-shirts clung to their chiseled chests as they discarded them, their jeans slipping down their legs like a tease, revealing the promise of what lay beneath.

Savoring the freedom, McDermott couldn't help but feel a rush of liberation as he shed his cum-soaked briefs, discarding the remnants of past encounters. The weight of expectation lifted from his shoulders, replaced by a blend of anticipation.

Their eyes locked once more, a silent understanding passing between them. Fortunato's playful wink ignited a fire within McDermott as if fanning the flames of their shared desire.

"I can't believe we're doing this," McDermott murmured, his pulse racing as he stood before the crowd, his naked form exposed.

"This is part of the job, kid," the older detective replied, his voice a low, seductive rumble.

"But, sir..."

"Trust me, McDermott. Let go. You're a cop. You gotta pass as a gay man, or we can't be undercover partners on this case. Don't think, just do."

"OK, sir," the young man nodded, his confidence growing.

"That's my boy," the veteran cop smiled, admiring the sight before him.

———

THE ROOKIE'S heart raced with excitement and nervous anticipation. McDermott couldn't help but feel a stirring in his loins, the undeniable proof of his arousal manifesting as a prominent, engorged nine-inch cock ready for action. His body betrayed him, the undeniable evidence of a desire on full display.

Ever the calm and collected guide, Fortunato leaned in close, his voice a low, seductive whisper that sent shivers down McDermott's spine. "Relax, kid. You're an absolute stud, and these men here... they're hungry for a cock like yours. They've been dreaming about wrapping their lips around your big, juicy cock, and now they can see it in person. Embrace it," Fortunato assured him, his words dripping with encouragement and sensuality.

A blush painted McDermott's cheeks, his gaze shifting nervously towards the expectant crowd. The notion of exposing himself so openly stirred a mix of embarrassment and arousal within him. "Sir, please don't remind me of that day in the locker room. It was embarrassing," he confessed, his voice laced with a hint of vulnerability.

Fortunato's fingers gently grazed McDermott's arm, a comforting touch that sought to ease the rookie's unease. "There's no need to be embarrassed, kid. We all have our moments of passion and desire. It's natural, human. We crave release, and there's absolutely nothing wrong with taking care of business," he reassured, his voice a soothing balm to McDermott's self-consciousness.

Gratitude washed over the young officer as he absorbed Fortunato's words. The weight of shame dissipated, replaced by a newfound acceptance of his desires. McDermott's blush gradually faded, replaced by a flicker of confidence that danced in his eyes.

⊂⊐

THE SEASONED DETECTIVE'S smile held a mischievous twinkle as he continued to guide his protégé. "Kid, getting an erection is a sign of your vitality and virility. It's a sign that you're healthy and alive. So, don't be ashamed. Embrace it. Revel in the attention," Fortunato grinned, his gaze devouring the rookie's impressive physique.

A flicker of realization dawned in McDermott's eyes, the realization that his arousal was not a cause for shame but a celebration of his desirability. A newfound confidence bloomed within him, a flame of self-assurance that burned brighter with every passing moment.

A nod of understanding passed between the two men, an unspoken bond forged in their shared journey of self-discovery. McDermott's lips curled into a smile, the weight of embarrassment lifting from his shoulders as he embraced the allure of the moment.

"Of course, you're right, sir," he acknowledged, his voice laced with a newfound confidence that echoed through the room.

Fortunato's chuckle rumbled deep within his chest, a gentle vibration that resonated through McDermott's being. His hand found its place on the rookie's shoulder, a gesture of camaraderie and support. In that touch, McDermott found solace, reassurance that he was not alone in this journey of self-expression and unabashed pleasure.

⊏⊐

"IT'S JUST strange being naked in front of a group. Shit, everyone's checking out your twelve inches, sir. It's like you're the star attraction here, dude."

The young officer's pulse quickened as he found himself bared to the world, his body a canvas of desire. McDermott couldn't help but notice the hungry gazes that trailed his every move, their intensity fueling the fire that danced within him. His twelve inches of raw masculinity commanded attention, a magnet for desire that left the room breathless.

Fortunato's laughter filled the air, a deep and throaty sound that mingled with the electric tension in the room. Alight with mischief, his eyes surveyed the crowd, reveling in the spectacle before them. "Well, kid, I can hardly conceal what nature has so generously blessed me with," he chuckled, his voice laced with a hint of playful arrogance.

A blush crept back onto the young officer's cheeks, his gaze shifting nervously amidst the sea of hungry eyes. McDermott couldn't help but acknowledge the truth in Fortunato's words. "If you've got, flaunt it, eh?" the young officer nodded, his blush returning," he murmured, his voice a mix of awe and self-consciousness.

Fortunato's grin widened, a glimmer of pride shining in his eyes as he absorbed the scene. "Exactly, kid. You're the star attraction; everyone here is captivated by your presence. They're entranced by your twelve inches of pure pleasure," he replied, his voice dripping with admiration and desire.

━━

EXCITEMENT AND UNCERTAINTY washed over McDermott, his body pulsating with anticipation. "This is so fucking hot, sir, but it's also strange. I mean, standing here naked, with all these men fixated on my throbbing cock... it's a bit intimidating," he confessed, his voice tinged with a hint of vulnerability.

Fortunato's gaze softened, a tender reassurance emanating from his very being. "Listen to me, kid. There's nothing to be intimidated about. You've been blessed with an extraordinary gift. Your cock is a work of art, a masterpiece that these men can't help but admire. Everyone secretly longs to experience the pleasure of your thick, juicy meat. But, for now, I'm the lucky bastard who gets to enjoy the privilege," he teased, his voice a seductive whisper that sent a shiver down McDermott's spine.

The young officer's confidence surged, a newfound embrace of his desirability. Once a source of uncertainty, the room became where his sexual prowess took center stage. McDermott's eyes locked with Fortunato's, a silent understanding passing between them.

"Sir, I trust you," McDermott replied, his voice laced with anticipation and surrender. The air crackled with electricity as their connection deepened, the promise of ecstasy hanging palpably in the air.

Fortunato's smirk grew wider, his eyes gleaming with a hunger that mirrored McDermott's own. "Good," he purred, his voice a sultry melody. "Because tonight, my dear rookie, we'll make this room come alive with pleasure. Every gaze, every touch, will be a testament to the allure of your magnificent cock. And I, for one, can't wait to savor every moment of it."

<hr>

"I'M NOT sure I can do this, sir," McDermott confessed, his voice tinged with uncertainty.

Fortunato's eyes bore into him, a mix of command and reassurance. With a firmness that brooked no argument, he commanded, "Hey, look at me."

McDermott's gaze met his, seeking guidance and support. He found it in the unwavering confidence that radiated from the older cop's every pore.

"You can do this," Fortunato affirmed, his voice a steady anchor amidst the rising tide of doubt. "You're more than capable, McDermott. You're a handsome, confident, and undeniably sexy young man. Own it. Show the world what you've got. Be proud."

The weight of Fortunato's words settled on McDermott's shoulders, infusing him with a newfound resolve. Gratitude filled his voice as he replied, "Thanks, sir. I appreciate the pep talk. I'm glad I have you here with me."

A mischievous grin danced across Fortunato's lips, his eyes glinting with a provocative spark. "But right now, McDermott," he purred, his voice dripping with desire, "I could use a blow job."

The young officer's breath hitched, surprise mingling with a heady mix of anticipation. "Sir, here? Are you serious?" McDermott's voice quivered with a potent blend of excitement and disbelief.

"Serious as fuck, McDermott," Fortunato replied, his tone leaving no room for doubt. "Get down and blow me."

———

A SURGE of heat coursed through McDermott's veins, his heart pounding in his chest. The gravity of the situation sank in, the thrill of the forbidden heightening his senses. With a nod, he acquiesced, his body moving with eagerness.

"That's my boy," Fortunato murmured, his voice a seductive whisper wrapped around McDermott. His hands guided the young officer's head toward his fully engorged twelve-inch cock, igniting a primal desire that surged within both men.

As McDermott's lips made love to Fortunato's cock head, a mixture of awe and excitement flooded his being. The world around them faded into a blur of anticipation, their connection becoming the sole focus of their existence.

"I can't believe we're actually gonna do this," McDermott murmured, his eyes wide, the electricity of the moment crackling in the air.

Fortunato's voice, filled with a raw hunger, echoed in the room. "Believe it, McDermott. Embrace the thrill, the intoxicating allure of this forbidden act. Let your inhibitions melt away as you indulge in the depths of pleasure that await us."

And with that, McDermott's lips parted, his mouth descending upon Fortunato's throbbing length. In that instant, they surrendered themselves to the currents of desire, their journey of pleasure unfolding with each tantalizing stroke, a testament to their shared hunger and the unspoken bond that drove them to explore the boundaries of their deepest cravings.

———

MCDERMOTT'S HEART raced in his chest as he took Fortunato's throbbing length into his mouth, his eagerness to please driving him forward. The taste of Fortunato's arousal, a heady combination of salt and musk, danced across his tongue, igniting his senses.

McDermott's lips enveloped the sensitive flesh of Fortunato's cock, his tongue swirling and teasing him. He reveled in the primal sounds that escaped Fortunato's lips—moans and gasps fueled his passion. His head bobbed in a steady rhythm, taking in as much Fortunato's length as possible, his lips stretching to accommodate the throbbing heat filling him.

Fortunato's fingers threaded through McDermott's hair, guiding and encouraging, his touch a testament to their trust and connection. McDermott's senses were alive with the intoxicating blend of power and vulnerability.

The room seemed to shrink around them, narrowing their focus to the sensations that consumed their beings. McDermott's cheeks flushed with anticipation and satisfaction as he explored every inch of Fortunato's arousal, his mouth and tongue working in tandem to elicit pleasured sighs and shudders.

Their connection deepened. McDermott's desire surged within him, aching for release and fulfillment. The taste of Fortunato, the weight of his need pressing against McDermott's tongue, drove him to new heights of arousal.

AS MCDERMOTT CONTINUED his passionate ministrations, his body burned with a hunger that demanded attention. The friction of his arousal against the roof of McDermott's mouth constantly reminded him of the pleasure that awaited him.

But in this moment, McDermott's focus was solely on Fortunato. He reveled in the power and control he possessed, his actions a testament to his dedication and willingness to go above and beyond the call of duty.

Fortunato's breath grew ragged, his grip on McDermott's hair tightening ever so slightly. Each flicker of McDermott's tongue, each gentle graze of his teeth, pushed them further toward the precipice of ecstasy.

⊏⊐

THE SENSATION of the young officer's warm, wet mouth enveloping his throbbing cock sent electric currents surging through the older cop's body. Anticipation crackled in the air, their desire intertwining like an unstoppable force.

"Fuck, that feels so good," the older cop moaned, the words escaping in a breathless rush as his fingers tangled in the young officer's hair. He surrendered to the pleasure, the tight grip of ecstasy building within him.

The rookie hummed, his tongue swirling around the tip with practiced finesse. Each motion was a testament to his skill and his dedication to the art of pleasure.

"Holy shit," the older cop gasped, his hips instinctively bucking forward in rhythm with the maddeningly sweet torment. An intoxicating wave of sensations crashed over him, propelling him further into sensual bliss.

"Mmm," the young officer moaned, his eyes closing, shutting out the world around them as he surrendered to their intimate dance. His lips, warm and eager, caressed every inch of the older cop's pulsating length.

"God, you're so fucking good at this," the veteran cop groaned, his grip tightening as his pleasure escalated. The young officer's talents were undeniable, his dedication evident in every artful stroke and sultry hum that escaped his lips.

"Mmm," the rookie hummed, his cheeks hollowing as he intensified his ministrations, drawing forth a symphony of pleasure from the older cop's depths.

THEIR CONNECTION INTENSIFIED, the air thick with the heady scent of desire. A group of men had gathered, drawn by the raw allure of their passionate union. Their eyes were fixated, captivated by Fortunato's impressive length disappearing into McDermott's eager mouth.

"Mmm," the rookie moaned, his hands skillfully caressing the older cop's balls, stimulating their electrifying encounter more.

"Shit," the veteran cop cursed, his body tensing as the pleasure coiled within him, threatening to unravel his self-control. McDermott's expertise was a revelation that threatened to push him beyond the edge of reason.

"Mmm," the young officer continued, his pace quickening, his eagerness matching the intensity of the older cop's mounting desire.

"God, that's so fucking good," the older cop growled, his hips thrusting involuntarily, seeking a more profound connection, deeper pleasure. They moved in a sensual symphony, each an invitation to surrender to the irresistible pull of their shared passion.

"Mmm," the rookie hummed, his throat relaxing, allowing the older cop to delve further into the depths of his being to experience the fullness of their connection.

"Fuck, I'm gonna come, man," the veteran detective cried out, his body shuddering with the overwhelming force of impending release. McDermott's skillful mouth had brought him to the precipice, teetering on the edge of an explosive climax.

"Mmm," the young officer mumbled, his eyes fluttering with a mixture of desire and anticipation, his own need echoing the older cop's.

"Ahh," the older cop groaned, his cock pulsing as ecstasy consumed him. The waves of pleasure crashed over his body, cascading through his veins, leaving him breathless and exhilarated.

"Mmm," the rookie sighed, his lips wrapping around the tip, savoring every last drop of the older cop's essence, a testament to their shared ecstasy.

"Fucking hell," the older cop breathed, his chest heaving with the intensity of their encounter. They had delved into the depths of desire, exploring the boundaries of pleasure with a fervor that left them both yearning for more. At that moment, as their bodies trembled with the aftermath of their shared release, they knew that their journey had only just begun, with a world of pleasure yet to be discovered.

"HOW THE HELL did you learn to give head like that?" the older cop asked, his eyes widening with astonishment, captivated by the young officer's skill.

"Lots of fantasizing, I guess, sir," the young officer replied nonchalantly, his voice tinged with a hint of mischief. He exuded a quiet confidence, aware of his power over the older cop's desires.

"Damn, kid. You're a fucking pro," the veteran cop grinned, his gaze locked on the sight before him. He appreciated the young officer's artistry of pleasure, a skill that left him yearning for more.

"What can I say? I'm a fast learner," the rookie shrugged, a playful smirk on his lips. His words carried an undertone of seduction, a promise of untapped pleasures yet to be explored.

"Well, damn. If that's the case, then you're going to be a great detective, McDermott," the older cop chuckled, his voice tinged with admiration and desire. He imagined the myriad of possibilities that lay ahead, both in the field and between the sheets.

THE SCENE HAD DRAWN the attention of several men, who couldn't help but show their appreciation. Their hands slapped the back of Fortunato in admiration, acknowledging the magnetic allure he exuded.

Fortunato, encouraged by the adoration surrounding them, pulled his partner closer, their bodies pressing against each other, their hard cocks grinding together in delicious friction. The heat between them intensified, an electric current of desire coursing through their veins.

"I think you're gonna pass for a pretty hot gay man, stud," Fortunato whispered seductively, his voice carrying a note of anticipation. "But I think you're gonna need a bit more practice. What do you say we head home for some late-night fucking?"

A surge of excitement shot through McDermott's veins, his heart pounding with anticipation. The prospect of surrendering to their shared desires was irresistible. "Lead on, master," he responded, his voice laced with desire. "I'll be your fuck slave all night, sir."

CHAPTER 4
LEATHER BAR FUCK

Det. Lance Fortunato and Officer Jake McDermott strode into the downtown gay bar. They were engaging in under-cover police work in the gay community in Boston. Fortunato had been slowly introducing the younger officer to various gay contexts to help him feel more comfortable in gay surround-ings and being among gay people. The hope was that he would be able to pass as a gay man by the time their case depended upon his ability to convince others of his gay identity.

Fortunato and McDermott commanded attention from the moment they crossed the threshold of the gay leather bar. Heads turned, gazes lingered, and a palpable energy crackled. The seductive beats of the music enveloped them, weaving through their bodies like an erotic current, while the vibrant lights painted their skin with a kaleidoscope of colors.

Fortunato stood tall and confident. His sleek, form-fitting leather outfit accentuated his chiseled physique. Every inch of his sculpted body was accentuated by the tight embrace of the garment, leaving little to the imagination.

A tight, well-worn black leather harness adorned his broad chest, the crisscrossing straps showcasing his defined muscles, pushing out his enormous pectoral muscles. The polished metal buckles gleamed under the dim lights of the leather bar, their presence adding a touch of dominance to his already commanding presence.

<hr />

HIS MUSCULAR ARMS were sheathed in black leather straps, making his biceps look unbelievably large, and the material hugging his skin snugly, emphasizing their strength and power. Each flex of his biceps sent ripples of desire through the crowd, drawing hungry gazes from those around him.

A pair of black leather chaps clung to his firm, exposing his naked rounded ass, molding to his every contour, clad only in a torn and ripped jockstrap. The cotton material whispered with every movement, hinting at the erotic secrets it held. The pants accentuated his long, powerful legs, their sleekness drawing attention to his every stride.

Completing the ensemble were polished leather boots that reached just below his knees. The sturdy soles provided a confident foundation as he navigated the pulsating energy of the bar, their gleaming surface reflecting the allure of the men surrounding him.

As Fortunato strode through the leather bar, his leather-clad body exuded a potent blend of confidence, allure, and raw sexuality. Every eye turned to him, their desires ignited by the sight of a man who fully embraced his masculine power and the seductive allure of the leather subculture.

MCDERMOTT ALSO COMMANDED attention as he entered the gay leather bar, his presence radiating strength and confidence for someone new to the gay scene. His attire, a compelling blend of leather and masculinity, accentuated his magnetic appeal.

Adorning his broad, muscular chest was a tight black leather vest, its intricate stitching tracing along the contours of his sculpted torso. The snug fit exposed his well-defined pecs and emphasized the power he held within.

Beneath the vest, McDermott was shirtless, highlighting his bulging biceps and sinewy arms. The smooth leather vest clung to his skin, accentuating every ripple and curve, leaving no doubt about the sculpted beauty beneath.

His waist was encased in tight black leather pants tailored to perfection to hug his firm, rounded ass. The material molded to his body like a second skin, evoking desire with every flex of his powerful thighs. The pants accentuated his commanding presence, exuding an air of dominance that enticed those around him.

Completing his ensemble were knee-high leather boots, their polished surface reflecting the ambient light of the bar. The sturdy heels added height to his already imposing figure, allowing him to traverse the space with purpose and allure.

Around his wrists, thick leather cuffs adorned his muscular forearms, symbolizing his submission to the intoxicating atmosphere of the leather bar. The metal buckles gleamed with a hint of danger, a visual reminder of awaited pleasures.

His leather-clad form exuded a potent blend of rugged masculinity and unapologetic sensuality as McDermott moved through the crowd alongside Fortunato. He became the embodiment of desire, drawing lustful gazes and sparking fantasies in the minds of those lucky enough to witness his commanding presence.

━━

THE AIR HUMMED WITH ANTICIPATION.

Fortunato and McDermott drank in the scene before them, their senses heightened by the intoxicating atmosphere. The crowd surrounding them was a mosaic of beauty and longing—an exquisite blend of masculine energy and sensual allure. They marveled at the diverse array of captivating men, each one a unique expression of desire. The air was thick with the intoxicating scent of cologne, mingling with the musky undertones of attraction, drawing them deeper into the night's activities.

Fortunato's charisma and McDermott's rugged charm became beacons as they moved through the crowded bar, casting a magnetic pull that captivated all who beheld them. Bartenders paused mid-pour, drag queens arched their perfectly painted eyebrows, and patrons leaned in closer to catch a glimpse of their presence.

Men of every shape, size, and ethnicity moved and mingled, each a unique expression of seductive allure. Their eyes roamed from chiseled physiques to slender frames, from smooth skin to tattoos that told stories of passion and rebellion. It was a kaleidoscope of captivating individuals.

As they ventured deeper into the throbbing heart of the bar, Fortunato and McDermott inhaled the heady scent of man musk. The air was heavy with the intoxicating aroma of cologne, mingling with the musky undercurrents of sweat and funk. It wrapped around them like an embrace, drawing them further into the captivating environment. The scent alone was enough to ignite their senses, fueling the fire of anticipation.

The music pounded through their bodies, vibrating with their racing hearts. Lights danced and played on their skin, painting them with dazzling hues. The vivid colors transformed their bodies into living canvases adorned in shades of passion and temptation. They moved through the crowd, their skin glowing under the flickering lights.

⸻

THE BARTENDERS behind the counter couldn't help but steal glances at Fortunato, their eyes lingering on his sculpted physique and how his leather harness clung to his taut, hairy muscles. He was pure leather daddy material. He exuded a confidence that was impossible to ignore.

It was as if a magnetic force emanated from him, pulling people closer, yearning to know him on a sexual level. His bare hairy ass was exposed by his jock under his chaps, and more than one person at the bar copped a feel as he walked through the crowd.

With his rugged good looks and smoldering eyes, McDermott had a presence that commanded attention. Patrons turned their heads to catch a glimpse of him, captivated by the intensity that radiated from within. His rough exterior held an irresistible allure, a mysterious charm that beckoned others to unravel the layers of his soul.

⸻

MCDERMOTT'S BODY was aflame with desire. "How far are you willing to go tonight, stud?" Fortunato breathed into McDermott's ear, his warm breath caressing his skin.

Caught off guard by the question, McDermott's voice trembled with excitement and curiosity. "What do you mean, Fortunato?"

A mischievous grin danced across Fortunato's lips as he leaned in closer, his eyes smoldering with an irresistible intensity. "I want you to push your limits, my stud officer," he whispered, his voice laced with a seductive edge. "Let's see what you're made of."

McDermott's pulse quickened, his body tingling with a heady blend of apprehension and eagerness. Without hesitation, he met the detective's gaze, his eyes filled with a fiery determination. "Anything, Fortunato. I'm ready."

Fortunato's approving nod ignited a surge of adrenaline within McDermott's veins. "Good," he murmured, his voice dripping with authority. "You'll let me know when you've hit your limit."

McDermott's lips parted in a breathless gasp, his imagination running wild with the possibilities before them. "Yes, sir!" he replied, his voice a blend of obedience and anticipation.

FORTUNATO'S VOICE took on a commanding tone, sending McDermott's heart into a frenzy. "Now, we're gonna start with a simple exercise," he instructed, his words laced with a promise of forbidden pleasure. "I'm going to walk away to the bar. When I'm gone, find the hottest guy in the place and kiss him. Not a peck, my dear friend, but a full-on, tongue-in-mouth deep kiss. You got it?"

McDermott's eyes widened at the audacity of the request, a thrilling surge of boldness coursing through his veins. "Yes, sir," he responded, his voice filled with excitement and determination.

Fortunato leaned in closer, his voice a velvety whisper that sent McDermott's senses into overdrive. "And make sure he knows you're with me," he added, igniting a delicious thrill in McDermott's core. "That'll turn him on even more."

A surge of desire mingled with McDermott's racing heartbeat as he absorbed Fortunato's guidance. He nodded, his eyes gleaming with a newfound confidence. "Yes, sir," he affirmed, his voice a low, husky murmur.

With a final, lingering gaze, Fortunato released McDermott from his presence, allowing him to explore any kinky desires he might have. McDermott felt a surge of exhilaration as he watched Fortunato retreat, his heart pounding in anticipation of the encounter that awaited him.

⊂⊐

FORTUNATO DISAPPEARED INTO THE CROWD. McDermott was left standing there, his heart pounding in his chest. He looked around the bar, his eyes darting from man to man. He saw a group of guys by the pool tables. They were laughing and drinking, enjoying each other's company.

Driven by passion and surrender, McDermott set forth on his assigned task. As he navigated the sea of bodies, the air crackled with electric energy; his gaze fixated on the captivating men surrounding him. McDermott's confidence grew with each step, fueled by the knowledge that he was carrying out Fortunato's command.

And then, like a predator honing in on its prey, McDermott's eyes locked onto the most alluring man within his sight. A magnetic force drew the two men together, their gazes sharing an understanding of the erotic dance about to unfold.

As McDermott closed the distance, his heart pounded in his chest, mirroring the pulsating rhythm of the music that enveloped them. He reached out with courage, capturing the stranger's attention. And at that moment, with a hunger that could not be contained, McDermott ignited a passion between them.

He walked over, his pulse quickening with each step. As he

approached, the man turned and looked at him. Their eyes roamed each other's bodies, taking in their muscular frames.

⸺

"HEY THERE, HANDSOME," the handsome man greeted McDermott, his voice dripping with seduction.

A surge of excitement coursed through McDermott's veins as his gaze met the man's intense, smoldering eyes. "Hi," he replied, his voice betraying a hint of nervous anticipation.

"You looking for some company?" he asked, his voice laced with a magnetic charm that sent shivers down McDermott's spine.

McDermott's pulse quickened, his inhibitions fading as a newfound boldness took hold. With a playful glimmer in his eyes, he confessed, "Actually, I'm looking for someone to kiss."

The first man's lips curled into a knowing grin, his desire mirroring McDermott's own. "Oh, really? Well, I'm always up for a kiss," he purred, his voice a sultry invitation that begged to be accepted.

The second man, unable to resist the allure of the moment, chimed in with equal enthusiasm. "Me, too," he added, his anticipation palpable.

⸺

CONFIDENCE WASHED over McDermott as he took charge of the tempting situation. His voice, laced with desire, resonated with a commanding tone. "Well, then, come here," he beckoned, his words thick with anticipation.

With each step forward, the two men closed the distance between them, the air thick with an electric charge of desire. The intoxicating scents of cologne mingled with the tangy aroma of beer, enveloping them in an irresistible haze.

Their breath mingled, warm and tantalizing, as McDermott surrounded himself by the handsome man's captivating presence. The world faded into the background, leaving only the delicious tension between them.

A surge of anticipation surged through McDermott's body, his cock stiffening in response to the erotic dance that awaited them. With an unspoken agreement, their lips met, and time stood still.

The softness of their mouths became their goal. Their tongues entwined in a passionate dance, exploring the depths of their shared desire. McDermott savored the taste of their shared saliva, a heady elixir that fueled his hunger.

━━━

AS THEIR LIPS moved against each other, McDermott's hands roamed the other man's body, tracing the contours of his form. The heat of their bodies pressed against each other. McDermott surrendered himself to the moment, his inhibitions cast aside. The world around them faded into insignificance as the pleasure of their embrace consumed him.

After a few moments, the two men broke apart, their faces flushed and their breathing ragged.

"Wow," the first man gasped.

"That was something," the other agreed.

"Thanks," McDermott grinned, his dick achingly hard.

"Anytime," the first man said, winking.

"I should get back," McDermott said, his voice husky.

"Of course," the two men nodded.

"See you around," the man smiled.

"Bye," McDermott waved, turning and heading into the crowd.

His heart was racing, his mind spinning. He had just kissed a total stranger, and it had been incredible. He could still taste the man's lips, his tongue. He joined Fortunato, who was watching him from the bar.

"YOU DID GOOD, man. Congratulations. Job well done. Now I want you to go over to that stud against the wall and grind him and let him feel up your rock-hard cock. And don't come back until you get him to stick his hand down your pants and grab your cock and pleasure you. Let me open your leather pants for everyone to see your hairy pubes as you walk across the bar."

McDermott followed Fortunato's gaze and spotted a tall, dark-haired man leaning against the far wall. He was dressed in a tight-fitting T-shirt and jeans, his muscular arms folded across his chest. His face was chiseled and handsome, his eyes piercing.

"Him?" McDermott asked.

"Yep. Go get him, dude," Fortunato grinned.

"Okay," McDermott nodded, his stomach fluttering. He was enjoying his training with Fortunato.

He made his way through the bar crowd, his eyes fixed on the man. As he approached, the guy glanced his way, a smirk on his lips.

"Hey," McDermott said, his voice barely audible over the thumping beat.

"Hey," the guy replied.

"I need to rub on you. That OK with you, man?"

"Sure thing, stud," the guy shrugged.

"Awesome," McDermott grinned, moving close.

MCDERMOTT'S BODY pressed against the other man's, their proximity electrifying. The mingling scents of cologne and a faint trace of sweat enveloped them, heightening the primal desire that crackled between them.

As the tension escalated, McDermott felt the man's gaze fixating on his rock-hard cock, reflecting his arousal. The stranger couldn't help but voice his admiration, his words laced with astonishment. "Damn, boy, you're packing quite a lot," he whispered, his voice a husky caress against McDermott's ear.

McDermott's heart raced in his chest, his pulse echoing in his ears. The stranger's words fueled the fire within him, a testament to their undeniable chemistry.

A mischievous smile curved McDermott's lips as he responded, his voice laced with confidence. "Thanks," he murmured, his voice a seductive invitation that conveyed his hunger for more.

The stranger, emboldened by McDermott's response, dared to venture further. His words dripped with a suggestive allure, tempting McDermott with the promise of unbridled pleasure. "You wanna let me in those tight leather pants of yours, dude?" he asked, his voice a low, enticing growl.

MCDERMOTT'S PULSE QUICKENED, desire pooling in his core. He met the stranger's gaze with a knowing look, his eyes sparkling with playfulness. "Help yourself, stud," he replied, inviting him to explore the depths of their shared desire.

A low moan escaped the stranger's lips as his hand slipped inside McDermott's trousers, his touch igniting a surge of electric pleasure. His fingers cupped the bulge, reveling in the hardness beneath his grasp. McDermott's body responded instinctively, arching into the touch, craving more.

The sensation sent shivers of ecstasy coursing through McDermott's veins as he surrendered himself to the stranger's touch. A sigh escaped his lips, his body a canvas for the stranger's exploration. "Yeah," he breathed, his voice a husky melody that mirrored the pleasure that surged through him.

The stranger's words, filled with awe and desire, stoked the fire that burned within McDermott. His fingers traced the contours of the thick, meaty shaft, reveling in the intoxicating sensation. McDermott's breath hitched with each stroke, his body responding eagerly to the stranger's skilled touch.

THE MUTUAL APPRECIATION of their endowed assets fueled their desire, each reveling in the other's glory. McDermott's hips swayed, grinding against the stranger's hand, his cock pulsating with unrestrained need. "You're so hot, man," the stranger moaned as he felt up the officer's fully engorged and hot cock.

A grin played upon McDermott's lips as he responded to the stranger's provocative remark. "So are you, stud," he groaned, his voice thick with desire. He reveled in the knowledge that their encounter was a dance of equals, a collision of two magnetic forces.

The stranger's smirk deepened, his hunger reflected in his eyes. "You like that, huh?" he teased, his words laced with a seductive edge.

"Hell yeah," McDermott growled, his voice a primal declaration of pleasure. Every nerve in his body hummed with anticipation, his balls aching with an insatiable craving for release.

The stranger's hands remained relentless, their exploration driving McDermott to new heights of ecstasy. McDermott's breath hitched as the stranger deftly worked to undo the button and zipper of his pants, eager to unveil the prize that lay concealed within.

An exclamation of awe escaped the stranger's lips as his eyes widened, feasting upon the sight before him. McDermott's confident chuckle filled the air, his satisfaction evident. "Like what you see, huh?" he purred, his voice a velvety invitation that lured the stranger deeper into their intimate embrace.

The stranger nodded eagerly, his hand wrapping around the thick, veiny shaft, reveling in its weight and hardness. McDermott's breath caught in his throat at the contact, a surge of pleasure coursing through him.

⸺

"MMM, THAT WAS GREAT," McDermott moaned before tugging his fat cock into his leather pants. "Thanks, dude. 'Preciate it," he said before returning to Fortunato at the bar.

"Dude, you got him to pull down your leather pants in public. You really scored on that one," Fortunato was beaming.

"I was nervous, but once I started, I was fine," McDermott confessed.

"You did great, and I'm proud of you, McDermott," Fortunato said as he kissed the younger officer as the stud against the wall watched them from afar.

"Now for your last exercise of the day. Pick the hottest guy in the bar to invite home with us for a three-way, all-night fuck fest. Wadda say?"

"Oh, hell, yeah," McDermott responded.

Out of nowhere, the two studs both stared at the hottest bartender either had ever seen. He was topless, and his body rivaled Fortunato's for the amount of ripped muscles. Both men walked over to the bar, and when the bartender leaned over to ask them what they wanted, Fortunato yelled in his ear, "I want my twelve-inch cock up your ass, and then I wanna watch you fuck my buddy here. What time do you get off, stud."

The bartender stud smiled and replied, "I guess I'm clocking off right now since I'm the owner. Let's take off, gentlemen."

Fortunato and McDermott were blown away. This was gonna be a night the two would never forget.

CHAPTER 5
THREE-WAY WITH THE BARTENDER

When Detective Lance Fortunato and Officer Jake McDermott stepped through Fortunato's luxurious condo doors, anticipation washed over them. The bartender they had invited home, a handsome stranger named Mike, stood before them, his eyes filled with curiosity and desire.

The trio of hot and randy studs quickly shed their clothes inside the condo, revealing their naked bodies, eager and ready to embark on an exhilarating night of hot, steamy sex and pleasure. There was a palpable tension in the room, but this soon dissipated as the three men came together for a group kiss, hug, and communal cock tug.

Fortunato's voice, laced with authority and seduction, issued a command to the bartender, a promise of the pleasure that was to come. "OK, Mike, bend over the sofa and let me prepare your eager hole, allowing my partner here to slide his impressive nine inches into your hungry, tight ass."

Mike's breath hitched at the explicit invitation; his longing mirrored in his response. "Fuck, yeah, Fortunato. I'm all yours to dominate tonight, stud," he replied, his voice a mixture of anticipation and surrender. He positioned himself as instructed, his body a canvas waiting to be pleasured by the two stud partners.

Before diving into their shared passion, McDermott's voice, thick with desire, proposed his tempting offer. "Here, dude. I can't wait any longer. I want to eat you out, man, lick your hole, rim you, and chew on that sexy hole of yours. Spread those cheeks, bro."

⊏⊐

MIKE ATTEMPTED TO PROTEST, saying he was self-conscious and concerned about his sweaty and dirty ass. But Fortunato and McDermott, driven by an insatiable hunger, paid no heed to the barriers threatening them in their quest to eat Mike's ass. They each approached Mike with determination, going down on his ass with their lips and tongues, taking turns exploring every inch of his willing flesh and gaping hole.

As McDermott's mouth plowed into him, Mike's protests turned into moans and screams that echoed throughout the condo. The walls trembled with the intensity of their shared pleasure, the boundaries of their desires shattering like fragile glass.

"McDermott, damn, bro," Mike panted, his voice an admixture of awe and pure ecstasy. He could barely catch his breath, his body trembling with the aftershocks of pleasure that coursed through him. "If I had known you were such a slut, I would have invited you to work me over at the bar."

Fortunato's lips curved into a satisfied grin as he watched his partner satisfy Mike. He had come along quite well in the past few days from straight boy to gay whore. McDermott was gonna do fine as an undercover cop in the gay underworld. There remained a problem for Fortunato, however. The truth was that the detective was falling for the younger officer and falling hard. He tried to suppress his feelings, but his desire and love for this younger man grew stronger daily.

⸻

FORTUNATO LAUGHED. "OK, boys, enough talk. Time to get our fuck on," he demanded. His laughter reverberated through the room, a playful command that signaled the end of idle chatter. The time for action had arrived, and the air crackled with anticipation, heavy with the promise of unbridled passion.

McDermott and Fortunato locked eyes, their gazes smoldering with desire as they reveled in the knowledge that they would both have the privilege of claiming Mike's hot, seductive ass. Their hunger knew no bounds, and they yearned to explore every position, every angle that would bring them closer to the pinnacle of pleasure.

A low growl rumbled in McDermott's throat, his arousal palpable as he voiced his urgent need. "Bro, I'm so turned on; I really need to bust a nut up your ass," he confessed, his voice laced with longing and urgency.

Fortunato's response was swift and equally charged with primal need. "Me too," he affirmed, his voice thick with desire. The fire burning within him matched McDermott's intensity, their shared hunger driving them to new heights of passion.

Mike, drawn into the electric atmosphere that enveloped them, echoed their enthusiasm. "Let's do this, dudes. I need each of your cocks up my ass. I need you to both shoot me a load," he groaned, his voice a mixture of anticipation and surrender. His body throbbed, anticipating being thoroughly claimed by these two virile men.

⸻

DESIRE HUNG heavy in the air as Mike's gaze met McDermott's, his yearning clear as he sought permission to indulge in a tantalizing act of pleasure. "McDermott, eat my ass again. Get me ready for Fortunato's monster cock," he pleaded, his voice filled with hunger.

McDermott's response was immediate, his voice dripping with enthusiasm. "Hell yeah, Mike. Give me that tight hole, stretch it wide open, and let Fortunato and I ravish your hot, sexy ass. We're gonna fuck you like you'll never forget."

Fortunato, driven by the same hunger that consumed them all, wasted no time echoing his agreement. "That's precisely what I had in mind, McDermott. Let's make it happen," he declared, his voice a potent mix of command and desire.

With eager determination, Mike positioned himself, allowing McDermott's tongue to explore the contours of his inviting moist ass. Every flick, every swirl of his skilled tongue elicited moans of pleasure from the bartender, his arousal growing with each passing moment.

The officer's mouth became pleasure Mike's ass as Fortunato grabbed some lube from his side table. Mike watched in awe as he witnessed the detective coat his twelve-inch fully engorged tool with Gun Oil lubricant. "Fuck," was all he could say as he began shivering in anticipation of receiving two hot cocks in one evening.

FORTUNATO, unable to contain his desire any longer, found solace in his touch. His hand wrapped around his throbbing length, stroking with an enthusiasm that matched the passion unfolding before him. Every stroke brought him closer to the edge, his pleasure mingling with the symphony of moans and wet sounds that filled the room.

The scene before them grew increasingly intense, a tableau of wanton pleasure that pushed boundaries and shattered inhibitions. Fortunato's suggestion was a plea, drawing all three men into a web of pleasure. "Bro, I've got to get my dick in your hole, dude."

Mike, his eyes glazed with lust, could only nod his agreement. He was beyond words, his body quivering with the anticipation and the sheer joy of knowing his ass was about to be claimed by two hot, horny, dominant cops.

Fortunato, his hunger reaching a fever pitch, moved behind Mike and slid his massive cock deep into the bartender's eager hole. "Fuck, yes, Fortunato. That feels so good, man," the bartender gasped, his voice thick with pleasure.

Mike's head snapped back, his eyes rolling into the back of his head, his body overwhelmed by the sensation. The feeling was indescribable, and he felt his orgasm building, his balls tightening, and his cock throbbing.

"Damn, dude, your ass is so fucking tight," Fortunato moaned, his voice a blend of surprise and pure delight. This was not the first time he had fucked a guy, but this was the first time the experience had been this intense.

"It's because your cock is so fucking big, man," Mike replied, his words a combination of awe and satisfaction.

⊏⊐

"I DON'T THINK it's just the size, bro," McDermott interjected, his voice thick with admiration.

"I'm not sure, either, but whatever it is, I'm enjoying the hell out of it," Mike responded, his words a mixture of wonderment and gratitude.

"So am I," Fortunato agreed, his words a testament to their shared pleasure.

"Me, too," McDermott said, his tone conveying his approval.

"Good," the bartender said, his voice a blend of amusement and satisfaction. Give me your cock to suck on McDermott. All three men smiled as McDermott repositioned and slid his cock down Mike's eager and open mouth.

"Now, let's fuck," Fortunato commanded, his words a declaration that the time had come for the trio's fuckfest to commence.

<hr />

AND SO, the dance began, the rhythmic thrusts and strokes a perfect harmony, the pace and intensity increasing as the men sought their release. They were lost in their world, their senses heightened and attuned to the sensations flowing through them.

"Holy shit, man. You're so fucking tight, and your cock is huge," McDermott murmured, his voice a combination of wonder and appreciation.

"I know, right?" Fortunato agreed, his tone a reflection of his astonishment.

"You're both pretty damn big, yourselves," the bartender countered, his words a testament to the pleasure the men were experiencing.

"Yeah, we are," the officers acknowledged, their voices a chorus of pride and accomplishment.

"Keep fucking me, guys. Fuck me harder," the bartender begged, his words a plea for more.

"Oh, we will," the officers promised, their words a vow that the night was far from over.

"Fuck, yes, keep going," the bartender encouraged, his tone a blend of encouragement and gratitude.

"Don't worry, we will," the officers reassured, their voices a pledge that the night would continue until the dawn.

<hr />

"OH, man, I can feel it building," the bartender warned, his voice laced with urgency and desperation, a potent mixture of pleasure and impending release.

"We're right there with you," the officers said, their voices resonating with the moment's intensity, a testament to the pleasure coursing through their bodies.

Ecstasy surged through the bartender, his cries reaching a crescendo of raw emotion. "Fuck, oh, fuck," he exclaimed, his voice a symphony of rapture, each sound a note in the composition of his pleasure.

The officers, caught in the throes of their ecstasy, grunted in unison, their voices a harmonious duet of bliss. "Fuck, yeah," they groaned, their words affirming the pleasure that enveloped them.

The bartender's voice soared, a cry of unadulterated pleasure that echoed through the room. "Ah, ah, ah," he screamed, his voice an anthem of euphoria, each syllable a testament to the pleasure that consumed him.

A chorus of moans and gasps filled the air as the officers joined in the sounds of pleasure. "Oh, god," they moaned, their voices a melodic hymn to the sensations coursing through their bodies.

<hr />

THE BARTENDER'S CLIMAX APPROACHED, a

wave of intensity crashing over him. "Fuck," he roared, his voice a primal roar, uncontainable and powerful.

The officers, too, could feel their release building, their voices mirroring their impending ecstasy. "Shit," they grunted, their words a primal bellow, manifesting their primal urges.

"Yes," the bartender hissed, his voice a seductive hiss, a serpent of desire coiled within him. "I'm gonna explode, dudes."

"Us, too," the officers growled, their voices a fierce growl, a pack of wolves ready to unleash their pleasure upon the world.

The bartender groaned, his voice a deep rumble like a bear awakening from hibernation. "Ah," he groaned, his voice a primal sound of satisfaction.

The officers sighed, their voices soft and gentle as a dove's coo. "Oh," they sighed, their words a delicate melody of contentment.

"God," the bartender whimpered, his voice a vulnerable whimper, a plea for release and fulfillment.

"Damn," the officers whispered, their voices a gentle murmur, a secret shared between them.

"Fuck," the bartender shouted, his voice a powerful roar, a dragon claiming its territory.

FORTUNATO SCREAMED OUT IN ECSTASY, his voice cutting through the air as he withdrew his massive cock from Mike's ass, his release painting the muscular man's heaving chest in a glorious display of lust fulfilled.

"Fuck," McDermott yelled, his voice a thunderous exclamation as he pulled his equally impressive nine-inch pole from the bartender's mouth, his climax decorating his face in a glistening testament to their shared passion.

The bartender's breath caught, his voice a hushed whisper of awe. "Wow," he breathed, his tone filled with awe and satisfaction.

"That was beyond amazing," the officers sighed, their voices a harmonious duet of appreciation, their words an acknowledgment of the pleasure they had shared.

"It truly was," the bartender agreed, his voice reflecting his satisfaction. "And now, it's my turn, studs. I can't hold back any longer, men."

"Go ahead, bro. Let it all go, dude," the officers encouraged the dude.

The bartender's warning pierced the air, his voice a triumphant blast like a trumpet announcing his impending release. "Here it comes," he declared, his voice filled with anticipation and pleasure.

"Yes," the officers cheered, their voices a resounding chorus of celebration, a choir heralding the arrival of his climax.

"Fuck," the bartender cried, his voice a cathartic wail, a release of pent-up desire and pleasure.

"Yes," the officers cheered, their voices a triumphant fanfare, a celebration of their shared pleasure.

"Oh," the bartender sobbed, his voice a mournful lament.

⸻

"THANK YOU, MEN," the bartender purred, his voice a soft, seductive murmur that lingered in the air.

"Hey, you're more than welcome, bro," the cops replied.

A sense of awe washed over the bartender as he marveled at the intensity of their encounter. "That was beyond incredible," Mike breathed, his voice a mixture of astonishment and profound appreciation.

The two cops nodded in agreement, their voices echoing his sentiment, a shared understanding of the passion and pleasure they had just experienced. "Absolutely," they concurred.

Exhaustion seeped into the bartender's voice as he confessed his fatigue, his words tinged with vulnerability and honesty. "I'm utterly spent," he admitted, his voice a whispered confession, as if revealing a secret desire.

The officers, too, acknowledged their weariness, their voices reflecting the toll of their intense connection. "We feel the same," they confessed, their words a gentle admission, a recognition of the physical and emotional energy expended.

FORTUNATO, ever the insatiable force of desire, broke the momentary silence. "Let's indulge in a well-deserved shower, men," he suggested with a mischievous glint. "I think I still have a few more rounds left in me tonight."

A renewed spark flared within the trio, anticipation mingling with their weariness. The prospect of further exploration ignited a fire of desire within them, fanning the embers of their passion. With shared smiles and eager nods, they headed toward the shower, ready to cleanse their tired bodies and embark on another chapter of their sensual journey.

The steam-filled room awaited them, a sanctuary for intimacy and pleasure. As the water cascaded over their exhausted forms, washing away the sweat and tension of their previous encounter, their bodies reawakened, tingling with the promise of new delights.

In the embrace of the shower's warmth, their fatigue melted away, replaced by a renewed energy, a hunger for more. The sound of rushing water mingled with their breathless gasps and murmurs, creating a symphony of desire that filled the space, heightening their senses and amplifying their connection.

⊏▭⊐

THE RIVULETS of water traced sensuous paths along their bodies, their touch gentle yet invigorating. Each drop became a tender caress, awakening nerve endings and reigniting the flames of pleasure that lay dormant within them.

As they explored each other's sculpted forms, their hands became instruments of pleasure, mapping every curve and contour, tracing the lines of desire. The slickness of soap and the intoxicating scent of passion filled the air, enhancing their tactile encounters and fueling their hunger for more.

Moans and whispers of longing mingled with the rush of water, their voices harmonizing in a crescendo of passion. The steam-clad room bore witness to their ardor, the air thick with the intoxicating blend of desire and steam.

CHAPTER 6
GAY MASSAGE

Detective Lance Fortunato and Officer Jake McDermott stepped into the clandestine realm of massage parlors, their pulses quickening with an intoxicating mix of excitement and desire. The alluring fragrance of aromatic oils enveloped the air, caressing their senses and luring them deeper into the seductive abyss. In the dimly lit chambers, secrets whispered, their hushed voices resonating with the thrill of forbidden indulgence.

Detective Lance Fortunato and Officer Jake McDermott stepped into the clandestine realm of massage parlors, their pulses quickening with an intoxicating mix of excitement and desire. The alluring fragrance of aromatic oils enveloped the air, caressing their senses and luring them deeper into the seductive abyss. In the dimly lit chambers, secrets whispered, their hushed voices resonating with the thrill of forbidden indulgence.

Fortunato finally felt that McDermott was ready to go undercover in their joint case. The two men had been working together for several weeks and staying together at Fortunato's condo. The two men would engage in constant sex when alone on the pretense of acclimating McDermott to the life of a gay man. Both men, however, were enjoying the process.

Each night, they would fall asleep in each other's arms, wake up the following morning, and have early morning sex. Fortunato was fearful that he was falling in love with the amazingly handsome and wonderful younger officer, and McDermott had begun to realize that he was, in fact, gay and that he craved to be in a relationship with Fortunato.

THE MEN HAD SPENT the last several days studying the local massage parlor industry and the clientele, focusing on gaining intel into one gay-identified business. They had learned the various code words and signals the employees and customers used, rehearsed and reviewed their respective roles, and discussed every possible scenario. They were as prepared as they were ever going to be.

Their mission was to infiltrate the underground world of gay massage and prostitution and, hopefully, find the source of the drugs distributed through the massage parlors. Over the past month, there had been a series of mysterious deaths from a new type of designer drug, a so-called 'super meth' or 'bath salts' that was rapidly becoming the new street rage.

As Fortunato and McDermott walked toward the front entrance of the massage parlor, their anticipation was palpable.

"Are you ready, McDermott?" asked Fortunato, his voice barely concealing his anxiety.

"I'm good," replied McDermott, his eyes twinkling mischievously. "Just relax and enjoy, Fortunato. I've got this."

⊏━━⊐

THE TWO STUDS arranged to go undercover as massage therapists with the establishment's owner. Fortunato would be the therapist, and McDermott would be his intern-in-training, acting as the detective's backup if anything dangerous happened.

"Here are your uniforms, gentlemen," the owner purred, his eyes dancing with mischief as he handed each cop a pair of tantalizingly skimpy white bikinis. The fabric felt like a whisper against their fingertips, a promise of the sensual encounters that awaited them. The air crackled with anticipation.

"What the hell is this?" Fortunato exclaimed, his voice laced with a mixture of surprise and disbelief. "I'm supposed to wear this? Are you kidding me?"

"No, my dear officer," the owner replied, his voice dripping with seductive confidence. "This is precisely what you'll be wearing. And, might I add, you're expected to stay in character."

A flicker of resistance danced in Fortunato's eyes, his discomfort palpable. "Customers expect this? Gay men are such sluts," he grumbled, his voice laden with a hint of frustration.

But McDermott, his partner, leaned closer, his voice a low, velvety purr. "Takes one to know one, eh, slut? I don't know. I think it's kind of hot," he whispered, his words laced with a mischievous wink that ignited a spark of desire between them. McDermott's playful confidence was infectious, a delicious temptation that beckoned Fortunato to explore his passions.

"You would," Fortunato laughed, a hint of admiration and longing hidden beneath the layers of his words. McDermott's audacity, his willingness to embrace the forbidden, stirred something primal within him.

―――

"WE'VE GOT a customer who is eagerly awaiting a massage," the owner interjected, his voice tinged with a knowing smile. "He's a regular, craving the touch of a couple of scorching-hot studs like you. He's not on your list of targets, but I thought you two might want to hone your skills and test the waters before your intended targets show up tomorrow."

Fortunato's gaze met McDermott's, a shared understanding passing between them. This was their moment to explore their desires and unleash the passion that simmered beneath their badges and uniforms.

"I suppose we're as ready as we'll ever be," Fortunato conceded, his voice a blend of resignation and curiosity. He shrugged, the weight of expectation slowly transforming into a heady sense of adventure.

A radiant smile danced upon McDermott's lips. "Let's do this," he agreed, his voice a low rumble of anticipation that ignited a flicker of heat in Fortunato's core.

―――

"ALRIGHT, gentlemen. Your customer, Alex, is waiting for you. He's a hot stud, a sought-after prize among the masseurs at the shop. You have the pleasure of his company for a full hour—make every minute count. We wouldn't want any dissatisfied whispers to tarnish our reputation."

Fortunato's lips curled into a confident smile, his gaze simmering with a promise of untamed pleasure. "Don't you worry, boss," he purred, his voice dripping with self-assurance. "We'll ensure that Alex experiences the heights of ecstasy."

A mischievous grin played upon the owner's lips, his eyes dancing with mischief. "That's precisely what I want to hear," he responded. "Now, go ahead and give him a massage he won't soon forget."

With a shared understanding, Fortunato and McDermott swiftly shed their inhibitions along with their clothes, slipping into the revealing and skimpy uniforms. What little fabric there was clung to their bodies like a second skin, leaving little to the imagination, accentuating every chiseled contour and sculpted muscle.

As they strode down the hallway, a current of electricity crackled between them, their eyes locked in an intense gaze filled with a fusion of determination and anticipation. Each step brought them closer to the room where their customer, Alex, awaited their touch—a rendezvous that promised to ignite fireworks of passion and fulfillment.

"ARE YOU READY, FORTUNATO?" McDermott's voice trembled with excitement and nerves, his gaze fixated on Fortunato's luscious form.

Fortunato met his partner's gaze. "Yes, I am," he murmured, anticipation coursing through his veins. "Let's have some fun as long as we're on the clock."

A flicker of amusement danced in Fortunato's eyes as he added, "And McDermott, do try your best to keep your arousal in check. We have a job to do, after all, stud."

McDermott chuckled, a low, seductive sound that resonated with the promise of forbidden delights. "Ah, but you know me, Fortunato," he confessed, his voice heavy with desire, "the mere sight of you in that bikini is driving me bonkers."

A blush tinged Fortunato's cheeks, a mix of flattery and excitement coursing through his veins. "Thank you for the compliment, McDermott," he replied, his voice laced with gratitude. "But don't lose sight of our purpose. We're here to give massages and fulfill fantasies for other men, not ourselves."

McDermott nodded, his gaze filled with a renewed focus. "You're right," he agreed, his voice tinged with determination. "Let's take care of Alex and his needs."

A shared nod sealed their unspoken pact, their hearts pounding in unison as they approached the door. The threshold of massage beckoned, and they were ready to answer its call.

⸻

THE TWO COPS entered the dimly lit room and were immediately assaulted by incense's robust and pungent scent. The room was sparsely furnished, with only a massage table and an open cabinet filled with various oils and lotions. A large, muscular man was sitting on the table's edge, his body completely nude with a visible erection.

"Good afternoon, Alex," greeted Fortunato, his voice slightly wavering. "My name is Fortunato, and this is my assistant, McDermott. We'll be taking care of you tonight."

"Hello, gentlemen," replied the customer, his deep, baritone voice sending shivers down the cops' spines. "I'm looking forward to a very special experience this afternoon. I'm really tense and want you guys to help me relax." Alex looked up and shuddered when he saw the two studs who were going to work him over. He had never experienced masseurs this hot.

"We'll make sure you have a memorable time," promised Fortunato.

"Do whatever you need to," smirked the customer. "I mean...whatever."

"Of course," said Fortunato, understanding the man's double meaning.

———

"ALEX, to start, please turn over and lie on your stomach, and we'll begin," directed McDermott.

"Sure thing, cutie," replied the customer, eagerly flipping onto his stomach, exposing a large, muscular, hairy ass that both cops immediately wanted to explore and play around with.

"So, Alex. You get four hands today. McDermott is interning with me this month. He's studying to become a licensed therapist and can't wait to get his hands on you. I mean...for the experience. McDermott, could you please start the music while I get the oil ready?" asked Fortunato, motioning his head toward the CD player.

"Sure thing, Fortunato," McDermott purred, his voice filled with anticipation as he turned on the seductive melody that filled the air. The pulsating beats resonated through the room, setting the stage for the sensual encounter unfolding.

"Nice choice," Alex remarked, his eyes locking with McDermott's, a knowing spark passing between them. The younger cop blushed, his cheeks flushed with desire and nervous excitement.

McDermott, with a confident stride, approached the massage table, his eyes fixed on the sculpted form of Alex, ready to indulge in the pleasures that awaited them. His hands glistened with warm oil, a shimmering promise of intoxicating touch.

"Ready, McDermott?" Fortunato's voice dripped with simmering desire, his gaze locked on the tableau before him.

"Yep," McDermott replied, his voice husky with anticipation as he positioned himself next to Fortunato.

———

WITH SYNCHRONIZED PRECISION, their hands descended upon Alex's body, their touch igniting a symphony of sensations. They moved as one, their palms gliding over taut muscles, tracing a path of irresistible pleasure.

"Ah, that feels so good," Alex moaned, surrendering himself to the intoxicating rhythm of their skilled hands. Every stroke and knead sent ripples of pleasure coursing through his body, unraveling the knots of tension that had plagued him.

"You're so tight, Alex," Fortunato observed, his voice a velvet whisper that sent shivers down the customer's spine.

Alex smirked, his eyes dancing with mischief. "Thanks, Fortunato," he replied, his voice laced with playful innuendo.

"No, dude," Fortunato continued, a hint of teasing in his tone. "I mean your muscles. They're really knotted up."

A knowing smile danced across Alex's face as he responded, "It's been a tough week."

"Well, we'll make sure you're nice and relaxed by the time we're done," McDermott assured him, his voice a soothing balm that seeped into the core of Alex's being.

"I'm counting on it," Alex murmured, his mind surrendering to the intoxicating blend of pleasure and tranquility that enveloped him. In the hands of these skilled officers, his world transformed into a realm of bliss, where desires were fulfilled and boundaries faded into oblivion.

AS THE MASSAGE UNFOLDED, a seductive tension filled the air, rousing a hunger that pulsed through the room. The cops' hands, skilled and daring, ventured beyond the traditional boundaries, guided by a shared desire to explore the depths of their customer's pleasure.

Their fingertips danced along the curvature of the customer's ass, tracing the outline of those firm, inviting globes. They teased the sensitive skin with feather-light touches, igniting a fire that spread like wildfire through his veins. The customer moaned as his cock throbbed and hardened with growing anticipation.

Alex's voice, a sultry whisper, caressed the air, "Mmm, that's nice." The customer's voice, thick with desire.

Fortunato responded, "Glad you're enjoying it."

"Oh, I am," he purred, his voice dripping with lust and need, surrendering to the intoxicating dance of pleasure that enveloped them.

His gaze smoldering with desire, Fortunato dared to push the boundaries further. "Would you like to focus on an inner ass massage for a while, Alex? Some anal work? It looks like your hole is puckering open and closed as if it wants some attention." Fortunato was laughing inside as he made the suggestion.

The customer's breath hitched, desire coursing through his veins. "Oh, god. Yes, please," he gasped, his voice betraying his need. "You studs are so hot. I really want you to work my ass, dude."

A chuckle escaped Fortunato's lips, a mix of confidence and anticipation. "Of course," he assured, his voice laced with a knowing tone that sent shivers of delight down Alex's spine.

MCDERMOTT, captivated by the scene before him, stepped forward, ready to fulfill their shared desires. "McDermott, can you please prep his hole a bit? Use some lube and stretch him open a little," he requested, his voice a low rumble filled with carnal hunger. "Then, I'll slide a finger inside him and a dildo."

"With pleasure," McDermott responded, his voice thick with anticipation, eager to embark on this journey of shared pleasure.

The customer's breath hitched, desire pooling in the depths of his being. "Mmm, sounds fantastic," he sighed, hoping that these undercover studs' skilled hands and insatiable appetites would please his needs.

McDermott's fingers gently probed the man's hole, slowly working the tight ring of muscle. He was careful not to hurt the man but also wanted to give him a thorough and pleasurable experience.

———

AS MCDERMOTT CONTINUED PROBING ALEX, pleasure washed over the customer, his body alive with electric desire. The room hummed with an intoxicating blend of tension and excitement, setting the stage for the sensual exploration that was about to unfold.

With careful precision, McDermott moistened his fingers with lube, ensuring a smooth glide that would ease the path to ecstasy. His touch was deliberate yet tender, his movements calculated to bestow pleasure and ignite a symphony of sensations.

The customer's breath hitched as McDermott's lubed fingers made contact with his most intimate entrance, sending a jolt of pleasure coursing through his body. A shiver cascaded down his spine, mingling with the growing heat that pulsed within him.

McDermott stretched him open with each gentle press, his fingers gliding with practiced ease, teasing the sensitive nerve endings hidden within. The customer's body responded, a symphony of pleasure and anticipation building within him.

A mix of pleasure and vulnerability intertwined as the customer's senses heightened. The slickness of the lube created a frictionless glide, enhancing the sensation of McDermott's touch as he ventured further, inch by tantalizing inch.

The customer's breath quickened, his heart pounding in his chest, as McDermott's fingers explored and teased, unlocking hidden depths of pleasure. Waves of sensation pulsed through him, his body aching for more as McDermott skillfully prepared him for the ultimate surrender.

MCDERMOTT'S FINGERS, drenched in lube, roamed with purpose. He varied his touch, employing various techniques to amplify the customer's sensations. His fingertips danced in circles, tracing patterns that sent shivers of pleasure radiating through Alex's body.

He applied pressure, his touch firm yet gentle, pressing against the walls of the customer's anal cavity. This deliberate stimulation awakened nerve endings, unlocking sensations that had long lain dormant and eliciting moans of delight from the customer's lips.

McDermott's fingers, nimble and dexterous, explored the customer's inner folds with precision. He sought out erogenous zones, stroking and caressing them purposefully. Each touch was a brushstroke of pleasure.

Not content with McDermott's fingers alone, Fortunato stepped in to introduce a dildo into the equation. Coated in lube, it became an extension of touch, a tool to elevate the customer's pleasure to new heights. With measured movements, the hunk of a detective gradually introduced the dildo, allowing the customer's body to adapt and embrace its presence.

━━━

AS THE DILDO SLID DEEPER, Fortunato maintained a steady rhythm, synchronizing with the customer's breathing and responses. He manipulated the angle and depth, seeking out those hidden sweet spots that triggered fireworks of sensation within the customer's core.

The customer's pleasure intensified with each thrust, his body a playground of heightened sensitivity and desire. Fortunato's every action was purposeful, calculated to elicit the most profound pleasure, and he reveled in the symphony of moans, gasps, and breathless pleas that spilled from the customer's lips.

Throughout the experience, Fortunato remained attuned to the customer's responses, his intuition guiding him to push boundaries and explore new vistas of pleasure. He adapted his techniques, varying the speed, depth, and intensity as he navigated the intricate pathways of the customer's desire.

The combined effect of Fortunato's touch, the lube-slicked fingers, and the arousing presence of the dildo sent the customer spiraling into a vortex of pleasure. Ecstasy and longing intertwined, building a crescendo that threatened to consume them all as they experienced a shared journey of passion.

━━━

"ALRIGHT, Alex. Here we go. I want you to turn over on your back and watch the two of us as we lube up our hot, erect cocks to massage your inner prostate, dude. Is that what you want from us, Alex?"

"Yes...yes, sir," Alex muttered as he repositioned himself. He was enjoying the show as the two hot cops stripped out of their string bikinis and lubed up each other's cocks in front of Alex.

"Holy shit, dude. How big is that dick of yours, Fortunato?"

"Only twelve inches. And judging by the plasticity of your hole, Alex, I sense that you'll be able to handle a good portion of what I have on offer," Fortunato responded.

"Oh, fuck yes, sir. Give me all twelve, Fortunato. I can't wait. You're such a fucking stud. I've only dreamed of being fucked by two hot studs like you guys. Please take care of me good and hard, men."

"Oh, we will, Alex. McDermott, you're nice and hard. Why don't you go first with your engorged cock, and then I'll follow," suggested the older cop.

"Sounds perfect," agreed the younger cop.

⸺

"PLEASE, HURRY. I'M SO HORNY," pleaded the eager customer.

"Don't worry, Alex. We're going to satisfy your every desire," assured the seasoned detective.

"Damn, your cock is enormous," gasped the customer, his eyes widening with anticipation as the younger detective's impressive erection came into view.

"Thank you, Alex," blushed the young detective, flattered by the compliment.

"Come on, McDermott. Take him," urged the experienced detective.

"Alright, get ready," said the young detective, his voice trembling with excitement.

"Oh, fuck! It feels incredible!" cried the customer, his body tense with pleasure as the younger detective's manhood slid deep inside him.

"You're so tight, Alex," groaned the young detective, overcome by the sensation.

"Mmm, ravish me, McDermott," moaned the customer, his body writhing in ecstasy, succumbing to pure bliss.

⸻

AS THE ENCOUNTER INTENSIFIED, the room filled with the scent of desire. The customer's hands roamed freely, exploring the muscular contours of the young detective's body while the older detective watched with hunger in his eyes as he reached out to stroke Alex's hard cock..

The younger cop matched the customer's fervor, thrusting deeper and harder with each passionate motion. Skin slapping against skin echoed through the room, mingling with their moans of pleasure.

"Fuck, you're amazing," gasped the customer, his voice filled with pleasure and surrender.

The older detective, unable to resist any longer, joined in, his experienced touch adding a new layer of intensity. His hands grasped the customer's hips, guiding their rhythm and amplifying the pleasure coursing through their bodies.

Sweat glistened on their skin as they continued their carnal dance, lost in a world of unbridled passion. "Yes, take it all," groaned the young detective, his voice thick with desire. He reveled in the tightness that enveloped his cock, urging him further into the depths of Alex's tight hole.

The customer's body quivered, overwhelmed by the sensations coursing through him. He surrendered completely to the pleasure, his moans growing more urgent and uninhibited.

Their bodies moved in perfect harmony, a symphony of desire and longing. The intensity built, pushing them both to the edge of ecstasy.

They climaxed together in a final crescendo of pleasure, their bodies convulsing with waves of bliss. The room was filled with their shared cries of satisfaction, their connection sealing their desire in a moment of pure pleasure.

As their breathing slowed, they remained entwined, bodies pressed together in a post-orgasmic embrace. The room was filled with a tranquil silence, broken only by the whispers of gratitude and contentment that lingered in the air.

⊏⊐

AS SOON AS McDermott's cock pulled out of Alex, Fortunato immediately inserted the tip of his monster cock into the client, who almost jumped off the massage table. "Holy Fuck, dude. Open me up, stud. This is a fucking dream, dude," Alex shouted for all in the parlor to hear.

As Fortunato eased himself into Alex's hole, each thrust communicated a sense of vitality, his desires intermingling with the electric energy in the room. It was a reminder of his sensuality and that he, too, was a creature of passion and pleasure. The customer's moans and writhing body fueled his arousal, their connection deepening with each intimate movement.

As Fortunato's hands guided their rhythm, he relished the sensation of control and connection. It was a heady mix of dominance and surrender, the boundaries between them blurring in the pursuit of shared pleasure. He reveled in the knowledge that he could elicit such fervor and pleasure.

As his climax washed over him, he relished his release, his body trembling with satisfaction. A sense of contentment settled within him in the aftermath, a profound fulfillment transcending the physical. He felt a deep connection with his companions, an unspoken bond forged by exploring their shared desires.

In the quiet moments that followed, as their breathing slowed and their bodies remained entwined, the older detective basked in a newfound sense of liberation and self-assurance.

<hr />

"ALRIGHT, Alex. Thank you for choosing us for your massage today. We're glad you enjoyed it, and we'd love to see you again soon," Fortunato said, a mischievous glint in his eyes.

"Oh, fuck yeah, count on it," Alex replied, a sly grin on his lips. He generously slipped a crisp $200 bill into Fortunato's hand, showing appreciation for the mind-blowing experience they had just shared.

As the steamy session ended, the two cops hastily tried to squeeze their sculpted bodies back into their snug work bikinis. With muscles flexing and the air thick with lingering desire, they exchanged a knowing glance, promising future encounters that would push the boundaries of pleasure even further.

Alex left, his body still humming with satisfaction, eager for the next chapter in their clandestine escapades. Fortunato watched him go, his gaze lingering on the tight, hot ass of the departing figure. He knew their paths would cross again, and the anticipation of future encounters sent a surge of excitement through his veins. The possibilities were endless, and they had only scratched the surface of the pleasure awaited them.

A lingering sense of fulfillment enveloped Fortunato as the door closed behind Alex. He knew their mutual desire would continue to burn, fueling their secret rendezvous in the shadows of their separate lives. Their paths had intersected, and now they were bound by an insatiable hunger that demanded satisfaction.

Fortunato and McDermott began to clean up the room with satisfied smiles, his thoughts drifting to the next client who unknowingly stepped into their world of seduction.

CHAPTER 7
GAY SEX SHOPS

Detective Lance Fortunato and Officer Jake McDermott stood at the threshold of Boston's alluring gay sex stores, their hearts pounding excitedly. This sexy world fueled their curiosity, as it could potentially hold the key to their investigation—the drug ring that lurked within its shadowy corners.

As the two undercover cops crossed the realm of temptation, a palpable charge filled the air, sparking their senses. Fortunato turned with concern to his straight partner McDermott and asked if he felt comfortable engaging in this seductive environment. McDermott's eyes scanned the shelves lined with bottles of lube and an assortment of provocative dildos, and without hesitation, he replied, "Hell, yes, sir." Fortunato couldn't help but smile, a flicker of hope igniting within him. Perhaps their professional alliance could evolve into something more—a passionate connection extending beyond their undercover operation's confines.

THE STORE BECKONED with its provocative display of pleasures and tools for fantasies. Each shelf boasted an array of seductive merchandise, enticing their gazes and whispering promises of unexplored delights. Vibrators, their shapes, and sizes as diverse as the desires they could fulfill, stood alongside leather restraints that hinted at the thrill of surrender. And amidst it all, tempting lingerie teased the imagination, fueling every gay man's fantasies of indulgence and seduction.

Fortunato and McDermott couldn't help but be captivated by the store's allure. Their eyes lingered on the sensual offerings, their minds weaving vivid images of the pleasures they could unlock. It was as if the very atmosphere of the store had cast a spell upon them, drawing them deeper into the web of desire.

The two studs knew that their journey within this intoxicating world was not just about the investigation—it was a chance to explore the depths of their desires and discover uncharted territories of pleasure. And as they stood there, side by side, their hearts beating in sync, they knew that their bond held the potential for a connection that transcended the boundaries of their profession.

With newfound resolve and a shared hunger for truth and passion, they ventured further into the store, ready to immerse themselves in a realm where secrets and desires intertwined. Little did they know that their undercover operation would expose the hidden underbelly of Boston's drug ring and unlock the door to a love affair that would forever change their lives.

AS THEY VENTURED DEEPER into the store, Fortunato and McDermott exchanged glances, their eyes meeting with a shared understanding. This journey was not only about their investigation but also about their desires. The boundaries between their personal and professional lives began to blur as the veiled world awakened something primal within them.

Fortunato and McDermott moved through the store, their bodies brushing against each other in passing, the contact sending electric sparks of desire through their veins. With each step, their connection grew stronger, their unspoken bond guiding them through the maze of desires and temptations surrounding them.

The two men wanted to assert that they were supposed to be perceived as a gay couple by being affectionate and physical with each other as they made their way through the store. At one point, McDermott reached out to grab Fortunato's hands, and as the two held tightly onto each other, the men looked into each other's eyes and saw more than a professional relationship. "Maybe this is actually going to happen," Fortunato thought.

▭

AS THE TWO studs approached a display of clips and clamps, McDermott was surprised to see Fortunato take his shirt off and tuck it into his back pocket. "Here, baby, let's try on some nipple clamps." McDermott immediately stripped his top off as well, and the two men began trying on the various clamps, the metal teeth nipping at their sensitive nips.

"Ouch! That's too tight," Fortunato said, wincing.

"Sorry, babe, I'll loosen it up for you." As McDermott gently adjusted the clamp, his fingers brushed against Fortunato's nipples, eliciting a soft moan from the detective.

"That's better," Fortunato whispered, his voice thick with desire.

McDermott's cock twitched at his partner's arousal, and he couldn't resist the urge to tease him further. He leaned in and flicked his tongue across the exposed flesh, the salty taste igniting his senses.

"Fuck, McDermott," Fortunato groaned, his body responding instinctively to the pleasure.

The two men's cocks strained against the fabric of their pants, their arousal growing by the second. They were both aware that the sexual tension between them had reached a boiling point, and they knew they would have to act on their desires at some point.

⸻

THE STORE'S air was thick with desire as men explored their hidden cravings. Bodies entwined, hands caressed, and pleasure filled the air like an intoxicating scent. The scene was an erotic playground where inhibitions were shed, and sensual possibilities bloomed.

Amidst the compelling displays, Fortunato's eyes locked onto McDermott with a hunger that couldn't be denied. He beckoned his partner closer, his voice a seductive whisper. "Come here, baby, and let me show you something," he purred, leading McDermott to a section of the store adorned with lubricants.

Curiosity danced in McDermott's eyes as he asked, "What did you want to show me?"

Fortunato's grin was wickedly enticing. "This," he replied, reaching for a bottle of lube. With a confident grip, he poured a generous amount onto his hand, the cool liquid glistening in the dim light. His gaze locked onto McDermott's, his intentions clear.

Without hesitation, Fortunato delved into the depths of McDermott's pants, his hand finding its way to his partner's throbbing cock. He slathered the slick liquid along the shaft, his touch sending shivers of pleasure through McDermott's body.

ECSTASY COURSED through McDermott's veins, his gasp of pleasure escaping his lips. "Oh fuck, Fortunato, that feels amazing," he moaned, his body quivering with delight.

Fortunato's voice, husky with desire, whispered, "You like that, don't you?"

"Yes, fuck, yes," McDermott responded, surrendering to the intensity of their connection.

McDermott's hips involuntarily bucked, seeking more of Fortunato's touch. The lube heightened every sensation, amplifying his pleasure. Fortunato's skilled hand stroked his cock, each stroke a symphony of bliss that pushed him further into ecstasy.

Their desires ignited, and Fortunato and McDermott were lost in a dance of passion, the world around them fading into insignificance. Their undercover mission became secondary to their raw, primal connection. Pleasure surged through their bodies, forging a bond that transcended the boundaries of their roles as detectives.

Within the store, Fortunato and McDermott embraced their desires, unashamed and unrestrained. Their bodies moved in harmony, pleasure building with each stroke, each caress. They surrendered to the intoxicating rhythm of their union, their private symphony of pleasure echoing through the store's hallowed halls.

THEY WERE NOT JUST undercover detectives on a mission. They were two men swept up in the throes of desire, finding solace and fulfillment in each other's embrace. And as they continued their erotic exploration, the boundaries of pleasure blurred, paving the way for a love affair that would forever alter the course of their lives.

Fortunato released his hand on his partner's cock and led him over to a group of studs rubbing dildos onto each other's engorged cocks within their pants.

"Let's get a closer look," Fortunato suggested, his voice laced with a hint of mischief.

McDermott's heart raced with a potent mix of excitement and anticipation. He couldn't believe they were about to enter this realm of forbidden pleasure. "I can't believe we're doing this," he muttered, his voice tinged with a breathless desire.

Fortunato's gaze burned with intensity as he leaned closer to McDermott, his lips grazing his ear. "Just go with it, McDermott. Let's have some fun," he whispered, his words unleashing a surge of electric anticipation.

Together, they closed the distance, their senses heightened by the sight of the half-naked, muscular studs entangled in their erotic dance. The air crackled with undeniable sexual energy as the men tantalizingly rubbed each other's rigid cocks through their pants, the friction arousing primal desires that pulsed within Fortunato and McDermott.

SUMMONING THEIR COURAGE, McDermott's voice trembled as he spoke. "Can we join in?"

A chorus of eager consent filled the air, and a stud, his gaze smoldering with desire, gestured for the two men to come closer. The invitation ignited a fire between them.

Fortunato and McDermott stepped into the circle, instantly enveloped in a haze of lust and desire. The scent of raw arousal hung heavy in the air, mingling with the musky scent of masculine bodies. Heavy breathing reverberated around them, a symphony of pleasure and longing.

As McDermott's fingers tightened around the offered dildo, anticipation coursed through his veins. The toy's weight in his hand hinted at the possibilities before them. With a grateful nod, he accepted the gift, his eyes meeting those of the stud who had offered it, silently conveying his gratitude.

The circle of men began to move, bodies grinding against each other in a primal rhythm, lips finding one another in feverish kisses. McDermott and Fortunato surrendered to the intoxicating atmosphere, their inhibitions melting away as they immersed themselves in this whirlwind of carnal desire.

Eager hands roamed freely, exploring the sculpted contours of bodies, seeking the pleasure hidden beneath the surface. McDermott's senses were overwhelmed by the touch of calloused hands against his skin, the heat of breath dancing along his neck, and the whispered moans of pleasure that echoed throughout the room.

———

"LET'S take this action to the back room, studs," one of the hunks in the huddle suggested, his voice dripping with desire.

The collective agreement reverberated through the air, a chorus of vibrant consent that set their hearts ablaze. McDermott's pulse quickened, his body responding to the primal energy that enveloped them. "Fuck, yes," he whispered, his voice laced with need.

Fortunato's eyes smoldered with a hunger that matched McDermott's. With a firm grip on his partner's arm, he urged him forward, their bodies moving together. "Come on, babe, let's have some fun," he suggested, his voice a seductive command.

McDermott's breath hitched, a mix of excitement and disbelief coursing through his veins. "Fuck, I can't believe we're doing this," he confessed, his voice filled with breathless anticipation.

Fortunato's voice dripped with assurance as he leaned closer, his lips grazing McDermott's ear. "It'll be worth it, trust me," he whispered, his words stoking the flames of desire that burned within them.

Following the group, Fortunato and McDermott ventured into the dimly lit back room, their senses heightened and their cocks pulsating with eager anticipation. The room was a sanctuary of hedonistic delights, where inhibitions melted away, and pleasure reigned supreme.

⊏⊐

AS THEIR EYES adjusted to the ambiance, a scene unfolded before them. The space was alive with the captivating sight of naked and partially clothed men engaged in a performance of sensuality. The air hummed with the intoxicating scent of musky sweat and desire, and passionate moans filled their ears, heightening their craving for connection.

McDermott's gaze roamed the dark room hungrily, taking in the diverse array of bodies, each a work of art in its own right. The sight fueled his fantasies, igniting a fire that demanded release.

Fortunato's hand found McDermott's, their fingers intertwining as they navigated the sensual dance surrounding them. With each step, they shed their inhibitions, surrendering to the allure of this clandestine world. Their desires mingled with those of the men around them, creating a tapestry of passion transcending boundaries and societal norms.

The store owner was in the back dark room and greeted the new customers by handing out free cock rings to the hot studs to wear.

With cheers, the men quickly stripped completely and began helping each other, getting their dicks situated in the cock rings.

"Oh, fuck, Fortunato, this cock ring feels so good," McDermott moaned, his voice thick with lust.

"Yeah, baby, I can tell. You were pre-lubed, so that made it easier to get this ring on your hard cock," Fortunato replied, his eyes raking over his partner's rock-hard cock.

———

THE ROOM PULSED with an electric charge as the two men moved toward the center, their bodies magnetically drawn together. A symphony of desire echoed around them, fueling their hunger for forbidden pleasure.

"I wanna suck your dick, dude," a beefy, hairy stud growled, his eyes blazing with need as he approached McDermott. The raw hunger in his voice sent a shiver of anticipation down McDermott's spine.

A wicked grin spread across McDermott's face, his desire matching the intensity in the stud's eyes. "Well, what are you waiting for?" he replied, his voice laced with a primal invitation.

Without hesitation, the beefy stud dropped to his knees, his tongue eagerly seeking contact with McDermott's throbbing cock. McDermott's breath hitched as the stud's warm mouth enveloped him, sending waves of pleasure coursing through his body.

"Fuck, that's good," McDermott grunted, his hips instinctively jerking forward, seeking a deeper connection. The stud's skilled mouth worked its magic, igniting a fire within him that threatened to consume his senses.

Meanwhile, a slim, young stud approached Fortunato, his eyes gleaming with lust as he dropped to his knees, his hands reaching for the detective's zipper. The air crackled with anticipation as their gazes locked, an unspoken agreement passing between them.

"Your turn, handsome," the twink purred, his voice dripping with desire. His hands worked deftly, releasing Fortunato's pulsing erection from its confines and exposing it to the air.

A mischievous grin danced across Fortunato's lips, his heart pounding with exhilaration. "Don't mind if I do," he replied, his voice resonating with a hunger that matched the twink's. His cock throbbed with eager anticipation, ready to be embraced by the young stud's skilled touch.

***

WITH A SURGE OF DESIRE, the two officers surrendered to the pleasure. Their bodies were pushed to the brink of ecstasy. In this moment, they were untethered, driven solely by the relentless pursuit of pleasure.

The room was full of intense sensations. Moans and gasps mingled in the air, creating a symphony of lust that echoed through the depths of their beings. McDermott and Fortunato, lost in their respective encounters, were swept away by waves of pleasure unlike they had ever experienced.

Time became irrelevant as the officers delved deeper into their desires. Each touch, each kiss, each thrust brought them closer to the pinnacle of ecstasy. Boundaries blurred, inhibitions shattered, and the intensity of their sexual encounters pushed them to new heights of pleasure.

They had entered a realm where pleasure reigned supreme, where their bodies intertwined in a dance of raw desire. McDermott and Fortunato embraced the moment's intensity, knowing that these were the most intense sexual experiences they had ever had and that they would forever be imprinted upon their souls.

———

THE AIR CRACKLED with primal energy as the beefy, hairy stud's mouth stretched wide around the cop's impressive girth. Pleasure and desire merged in a symphony of moans and grunts, filling the room with a heady atmosphere.

"God, your dick is fucking huge," the stud groaned, his voice laced with awe and craving. Every inch of him yearned to be filled, to succumb to the cop's commanding presence.

A feral grin curled on McDermott's lips, his hips thrusting forward with an irresistible force. "Yeah, and you're gonna take it all, aren't you, bitch," he growled, his voice dripping with dominance. The cop's desire surged through him, urging him to claim his willing partner.

"Mm-hmm," the beefy, hairy stud hummed, his throat muscles contracting around the cop's throbbing shaft. His mouth became a haven of pleasure, the perfect vessel to accommodate McDermott's relentless size. Every movement and every sensation intensified the connection between them.

The scene unfolded before Fortunato's eyes, his desire reaching a fever pitch. "Fuck, that's so hot," he moaned, his voice a mixture of admiration and arousal. Seeing his partner claiming the stud with such raw passion ignited a fire within him, demanding release.

———

A SLIM, young stud focused on Fortunato's cock, his skilled tongue tracing teasing patterns along the sensitive head. The detective's body quivered with anticipation, his senses heightened by the intoxicating pleasure bestowed upon him.

"Oh, god, I'm gonna cum," Fortunato cried out, his voice filled with ecstasy. The pleasure spiraled through him, threatening to consume his entire being. His body trembled with the intensity of the impending release.

"Do it, daddy, give it to me," the slim, young stud pleaded, his eyes sparkling with excitement. He craved the cop's essence, hungry for the taste of Fortunato's ecstasy. His plea was a siren's call, beckoning the detective to surrender to the waves of pleasure crashing within him.

"Fuck, yes!" Fortunato's voice rang out, a declaration of surrender to the overwhelming bliss. Pleasure surged through him as release washed over his body, his essence spilling forth in a symphony of pleasure.

The two cops reached their pinnacle together, their bodies shuddering in unison as they surrendered to the intoxicating pleasure. A moment of blissful chaos enveloped them, their shared release forging a bond that would forever be etched into their memories.

"Holy shit, that was fucking intense," the beefy, hairy stud panted, his chest heaving with exertion. The cop's body radiated with satisfaction and exhilaration, the echoes of their shared encounter reverberating through him.

"Yeah, it was," McDermott agreed, his voice husky and filled with the remnants of their passion. The intensity of their connection lingered, a tangible presence in the air. They had traversed a path of raw desire, and the memory of their encounter would long fuel their hunger.

CHAPTER 8
COPS IN UNDERWEAR

Det. Lance Fortunato and Office Jake McDermott left the back room of the Sex Store satisfied. The taste of their shared desire lingered on their lips as the two cop partners kissed, savoring the remnants of their passionate connection. With a knowing glance, Fortunato suggested a detour to the front rack of sexy underwear before their departure.

"Let's hit the front rack of sexy underwear before we leave, bro," he proposed, his voice carrying a hint of mischief.

"Good call, dude," McDermott agreed, his agreement punctuated by a nod. The anticipation of exploring the enticing display ignited a spark within him.

"Fuck, yeah," Fortunato said, his eyes brightening with excitement. The prospect of immersing themselves in a sea of seductive garments fueled their desires, adding a new layer of anticipation to their electrified bodies.

Feeling the pulsating energy between them, they stepped back into the central area of the store. Their presence commanded attention, their bodies still humming with the echoes of their recent encounter. The aura of their shared passion was palpable, drawing curious glances from others who could sense the raw desire emanating from the two handsome men.

"WHAT SIZE ARE you looking for, sir?" the salesman inquired, his eyes flickering with anticipation.

"I'm a large, dude. And I need an extra large pouch if you have any," Fortunato confidently replied, his gaze lingering on the salesman.

"I can see that clearly, sir. Okay, great. I'll grab a few things for you and some mediums for your stud partner here," the salesman responded, his voice laced with mischief. As he walked away, he couldn't resist the temptation, reaching out to tweak McDermott's nipples, leaving a spark of desire in his wake.

"Fuck, dude. What the hell was that all about?" McDermott questioned, his voice tinged with surprise.

"He's just messing around, man. It's no big deal. Plus, I know you liked it, right?" Fortunato retorted, a mischievous grin spreading across his face.

"Sure thing, big guy," McDermott chuckled, his laughter hinting at a hidden desire.

Excitement crackled in the air as the two detectives eagerly awaited the salesman's return. When he reappeared, he carried a selection of skimpy, revealing underwear, a feast for their hungry eyes.

"HERE YOU GO, fellas. These should fit nicely," the salesman declared, his gaze wandering over the contours of their bodies, his appreciation evident. "No need to use the fitting room. I think everyone in the store would appreciate giving you feedback on your selections. I tried to pick the most revealing items."

"Great, thanks, man," Fortunato acknowledged, a sly wink accompanying his words.

"My pleasure, fellas," the salesman responded, his eyes lingering on the bulges that strained against their pants, his desire palpable.

Unable to resist the allure of the moment, Fortunato felt a surge of excitement. He urged McDermott, "Come on, let's try these bad boys on," his fingers instinctively reaching to tweak a nipple ring on his chest, heightening his arousal.

"Hell, yeah," McDermott eagerly agreed, his pulse quickening with anticipation.

Stepping into the spotlight, the two men shed their clothes, unveiling their naked forms to the applause and hungry gazes of the men around them. Embracing the thrill of exhibitionism, they each selected a skimpy pair of underwear, their choices daring and provocative, promising to showcase their assets in all their enticing glory.

WHEN FORTUNATO and McDermott unveiled their provocative bodies, a hush fell over the audience, their collective breath catching in anticipation. All eyes were drawn to the captivating duo, their sensual energy filling the room, their exhibitionism pushing the boundaries of desire.

"Damn, son, those look fucking hot," a burly, bearded man exclaimed, his eyes fixated on the tantalizing sight before him—

the detectives' crotches tantalizingly outlined in the skimpy underwear.

A knowing smirk played across Fortunato's lips as he caressed his package, relishing in the attention. "You think so, huh?" he purred, his voice laced with seductive confidence.

"Hell, yeah," the burly, bearded man responded, his voice thick with lust, his desire palpable.

McDermott chimed in, unable to resist joining the enticing exchange, his hands boldly stroking his package. "They feel good, too," he admitted, his voice tinged with satisfaction and arousal.

"I'll bet they do," the burly, bearded man murmured, his gaze irresistibly drawn to the detectives' groins, his hunger burning in his eyes.

Fortunato, eager to tease and please, turned around, his gaze locked with the burly, bearded man's. "How's my ass look in these, dude?" he inquired, his voice dripping with playful seduction as he looked over his shoulder, inviting inspection.

"Like a fucking dream, bro," the burly, bearded man sighed, his voice filled with longing, his eyes devouring the sight before him.

⸺

A MISCHIEVOUS LAUGHTER escaped Fortunato's lips, his eyes gleaming with satisfaction. "You hear that, McDermott? We've got ourselves a fan," he declared, relishing in the admiration.

"I'll say," McDermott chuckled, his cheeks flushed with excitement and desire, caught up in the intoxicating web of attention.

Sensing the charged atmosphere, the salesman interjected, offering another skimpy pair of underwear. "Try this one on next," he suggested, his desire barely concealed.

"Why not," Fortunato shrugged, slipping the garment on, the fabric clinging to his body, accentuating every curve and bulge.

"Wow, those are nice," the salesman gasped, his eyes widening with appreciation.

"They're a bit tight," Fortunato remarked, adjusting his package, a hint of his arousal peeking out from the waistband of the revealing bikini brief.

"That's the point, dude. They're supposed to make your junk stand out," the salesman explained, his gaze fixated on the detectives' groins, his desire evident.

"I'll say," the burly, bearded man interjected, his voice dripping with desire, unable to contain his longing for the captivating duo before him. The air crackled with anticipation, desire intertwining with the promise of an unforgettable encounter.

THE SALESMAN, ATTUNED TO THE DETECTIVES' desires and eager to cater to their every whim, presented an enticing selection of underwear for their exploration. Here are some additional types of underwear he had for them to try on:

"Alright, gentlemen, I've got a few more options for you," the salesman announced, a glimmer of excitement dancing in his eyes. With a flourish, he revealed a set of daring jockstraps, their straps beckoning with a promise of revealing masculinity.

"These jockstraps are perfect for showcasing your assets," the salesman suggested, his voice laced with anticipation.

Fortunato and McDermott exchanged a knowing glance, their curiosity piqued. They eagerly took hold of the jockstraps, their fingers tracing the straps and imagining the effect they would have on their bodies.

"Damn, these are hot," Fortunato remarked, his voice filled with appreciation.

McDermott nodded in agreement, his eyes fixated on the alluring garment. "They leave little to the imagination," he added, his voice tinged with excitement.

Encouraged by their enthusiasm, the salesman continued his presentation, revealing a collection of sleek and form-fitting boxer briefs. The fabric whispered promises of comfort and sensuality, their designs emphasizing the contours of the detectives' bodies.

"For a touch of sophistication and allure, these boxer briefs are an excellent choice," the salesman suggested, his voice brimming with anticipation.

FORTUNATO AND MCDERMOTT eagerly examined the boxer briefs, their hands gliding over the smooth fabric. The thought of their bodies embraced by such sensuous garments sent a shiver of excitement through them.

"Nice," Fortunato murmured, his voice betraying his growing arousal.

McDermott nodded, his eyes filled with desire. "They accentuate every curve," he observed, his voice thick with anticipation.

Sensing their eagerness, the salesman couldn't resist offering one more option. With a flourish, he revealed a set of risqué leather briefs, their provocative design leaving little to the imagination.

"For those who dare to explore their wild side, these leather briefs are perfect," the salesman declared, his voice seductive.

Fortunato and McDermott's gazes locked onto the leather briefs, their eyes filled with desire and a hunger for adventure. The thought of their bodies adorned in such forbidden indulgence sent a surge of excitement through them.

"Fuck, these are intense," Fortunato breathed, his voice laden with anticipation.

McDermott's pulse quickened as he imagined the feel of the leather against his skin. "They scream raw desire," he admitted, his voice laced with apprehension and longing.

The detectives couldn't help but be captivated by the array of options, each garment promising its unique blend of allure and sensuality. With their hearts racing and minds ablaze with desire, they were ready to explore the depths of their fantasies, their bodies yearning for the transformative embrace of these provocative undergarments.

THE SALESMAN, eager to fulfill the detectives' desires, continued unveiling an irresistible assortment of underwear options, each designed to ignite their passions. Here are a few more options for them to explore:

"Alright, gentlemen, prepare yourselves for the next set," the salesman announced, a glint of mischief in his eyes. He revealed a series of sheer mesh briefs, their transparent fabric leaving little to the imagination.

"These mesh briefs are perfect for showcasing your assets while adding an element of teasing allure," the salesman suggested, his voice filled with anticipation.

Fortunato and McDermott exchanged a knowing look, their interest piqued. They eagerly reached out to feel the delicate mesh against their fingertips, envisioning how it would mold to their bodies, leaving little hidden.

"Damn, these are sexy," Fortunato remarked, his voice filled with appreciation.

McDermott nodded in agreement, his eyes lingering on the tantalizing fabric. "They'll drive anyone wild with desire," he added, his voice laced with anticipation.

Encouraged by their response, the salesman continued his presentation, unveiling a collection of strappy harness briefs. The intricate designs of the straps hinted at a world of pleasure and exploration, adding an edgy and provocative touch to their ensemble.

"For those who crave a taste of bondage-inspired sensuality, these harness briefs are a daring choice," the salesman suggested, his voice dripping with excitement.

FORTUNATO AND MCDERMOTT examined the harness briefs, their fingers tracing the contours of the straps, imagining the sensation of being both adorned and constrained by their seductive allure.

"Oh, these are intense," Fortunato murmured, his voice filled with intrigue and desire.

McDermott's eyes sparkled with a hint of mischief as he envisioned how the harness would accentuate their bodies. "They'll unleash our most primal desires," he admitted, his voice tinged with anticipation.

The salesman, aware of their growing enthusiasm, couldn't resist offering one final option. With a flourish, he revealed a selection of barely-there thongs, their minimal coverage leaving little to the imagination and promising an unbridled display of eroticism.

———

"FOR THOSE WHO dare to bare it all, these thongs are the epitome of seductive confidence," the salesman declared, his voice filled with a hint of seduction.

Fortunato and McDermott fixated on the revealing thongs, their eyes drawn to the tantalizing slivers of fabric. The thought of embracing such minimalism and their uninhibited desires sent a surge of excitement through them.

"Fuck, these are daring," Fortunato breathed, his voice filled with excitement and anticipation.

McDermott's heart raced as he imagined the provocative freedom the thongs would grant them. "They'll ignite a fire that can't be extinguished," he admitted, his voice laced with a hunger for exploration.

With each new option, the detectives' desires grew, and their boundaries pushed further as they considered the endless possibilities for indulgence and pleasure. The salesman's offerings had unlocked a realm of sensuality. Fortunato and McDermott were ready to immerse themselves fully, their bodies yearning for the transformative embrace of these daring and provocative undergarments.

———

"THESE BRIEFS ARE DEFINITE KEEPERS," the cops announced, their voices filled with excitement and anticipation.

"I couldn't agree more," someone in the crowd responded, their eyes lingering on the enticing display.

"If only we could test out their functionality, you know, slip our hard cocks out from the top and give them a proper test drive," Fortunato voiced aloud, a mischievous glimmer in his eyes. McDermott couldn't help but burst into laughter, thoroughly amused by his partner's bold suggestion.

Before they knew it, the air crackled with electric energy as two stunning studs shed their gym shorts and eagerly positioned themselves before the two cops, their inviting asses on full display.

"Well, well, that was easier than expected," Fortunato remarked to McDermott, a playful smirk dancing on his lips.

STILL CHUCKLING, McDermott pulled out his throbbing cock, the desire burning in his eyes. He reached for the bottle of lube resting on the counter, swiftly coating his impressive length before passing it on to Fortunato, who was ready to join in on the pleasure.

"Time to unleash our desires, dude," McDermott whispered, his voice laced with raw intensity as he positioned himself behind the beefy, hairy stud, anticipation coursing through his veins.

"Fuck, yes," the beefy, hairy stud hissed, his hips eagerly bucking, craving the connection.

"Damn, that's a sweet, tempting ass," the detective murmured, his strong hands gripping the stud's hips, guiding the rhythm of their union.

"You can say that again," the slim, young stud agreed, his eyes gleaming with desire, eager to witness the raw passion unfold before them.

━━

"I DON'T HAVE all day, stud," the beefy, hairy man demanded, his body trembling with desire. "Stick that thick cock deep into my hungry ass."

The detective shook his head, a knowing smile playing on his lips.

"Please, daddy, I need you," the beefy, hairy man pleaded, his voice thick with desperation, his eyes pleading for release.

"Well, since you asked so nicely," the detective responded, his smirk betraying his growing arousal. His throbbing member pressed against the entrance of the beefy, hairy man, teasingly nudging against his tight opening.

"Oh, fuck, yes!" the beefy, hairy man gasped, his hips instinctively arching towards the detective's touch, craving more.

"You love that, don't you, my eager bitch?" the detective growled, his fingers digging into the flesh of the beefy, hairy man, asserting his dominance.

"Yes, daddy," the beefy, hairy man panted, his body writhing beneath the detective's commanding presence, surrendering to the pleasure that consumed him.

"Beg for it, my insatiable bitch," the detective commanded, his fingers curling around the shaft of the beefy, hairy man, stroking him with purpose.

"Please, daddy, please," the beefy, hairy man sobbed, his body trembling as waves of pleasure surged through him, aching for release, his vulnerability laid bare before his dominant lover.

━━

THE DETECTIVE EXUDED an undeniable air of dominance, his commanding presence filling the room. As he towered over the beefy, hairy man, his gaze held a mix of authority and desire, captivating his submissive partner.

The detective's every movement was deliberate and confident, his body language oozing with self-assurance. His robust and chiseled physique commanded attention, his broad shoulders and defined muscles a testament to his strength.

His voice, deep and resonant, carried a subtle undertone of power. With each word he uttered, the detective's commanding tone sent shivers down the beefy, hairy man's spine, intensifying the erotic tension that enveloped them.

The detective's touch was firm and possessive, his fingers gripping the flesh of the beefy, hairy man with unyielding strength. Every caress and squeeze conveyed a sense of ownership, leaving no doubt about who was in control.

His dominant presence extended beyond physicality, encompassing a profound understanding of his submissive partner's desires and limits. The detective exuded an aura of dominance transcending the bedroom, permeating every aspect of their intimate encounter.

In the face of such dominance, the beefy, hairy man couldn't help but surrender, his body and mind succumbing to the detective's commanding allure. In this surrender, their desires intertwined, creating a powerful connection that fueled their passionate encounter.

⸺

"GIVE IT TO ME, BABY," the detective growled, his teeth sinking into the neck of the muscular, hairy hunk.

"Ohhh, fuck," the hunk moaned, his body trembling with pleasure.

"That's right, my dirty little slut, cum for daddy," the detective groaned, his throbbing cock releasing its load deep inside the hunk's tight ass.

"You were incredible, man," the hunk said, his voice husky with satisfaction.

McDermott reveled in the intense pleasure of his passionate encounter with the sexy hunk before him. As a man who had always identified as straight, he was slowly embracing the realization that his desires led him toward the authentic path of being gay. However, he hadn't yet found the courage to share this revelation with Fortunato. The fear of rejection from the man he was growing attached to, and perhaps even falling in love with, held him back.

For now, McDermott indulged in the thrill of public pleasure, cherishing the erotic excitement of their steamy rendezvous. Surrounded by a crowd of eager men, the two studs thrust and pounded, their bodies a spectacle for all to witness. Nipple rings were teased, fingers slipped into hungry asses, and every man's throbbing member was fully exposed. It was evident that the two willing recipients of pleasure would soon become a collective vessel of satisfaction, eagerly embracing the deluge of cum from everyone present in the store.

⸻

THE SCENE UNFOLDED before the rapt audience. Sweat and sex mingled, creating an intoxicating aroma that hung in the air. Moans and gasps filled the space, blending with the slapping of flesh on flesh.

Around the two studs, men were consumed by an insatiable hunger, their eyes gleaming with lust and anticipation. They watched as McDermott and the hunk surrendered their bodies to pleasure, becoming vessels of sensual satisfaction.

The onlookers, unable to resist the magnetic pull of the erotic spectacle, could no longer contain their desires. Men reached between their legs, stroking themselves with abandon, their breaths ragged and heavy. Some couldn't resist the temptation to touch one another, their hands exploring the contours of willing bodies nearby.

The atmosphere was electric, charged with a primal energy that drew everyone closer. The store became a sanctuary of unbridled hedonism, where inhibitions crumbled and desires ran free. It was a moment of shared ecstasy, where boundaries blurred, and the collective pursuit of pleasure united the men in a powerful, unspoken bond.

The anticipation peaked as McDermott and the hunk embraced their roles as willing recipients. The crowd, now a sea of pulsating desire, closed in, eager to partake in the culmination of their shared passion. They became a chorus of moans and whispers, their voices blending into a symphony of pleasure.

In that explosive moment, McDermott and the hunk became the focal point of an unrelenting storm of pleasure. Every man in the store became a participant, joining together to unleash their emotional desires upon the willing bodies that offered themselves so willingly. The store transformed into a sanctuary of blissful release as the studs became a magnificent cum dump, accepting the offerings of ecstasy from their fellow men with open arms and insatiable hunger.

"OH, FUCK, THIS IS INTENSE," McDermott's playmate moaned, their hips grinding together in a feverish rhythm.

"Damn, I'm so close," McDermott grunted, feeling the throbbing anticipation building in his cock.

"Me too," his eager partner whimpered, their muscles taut with insatiable desire.

"Cum for me, you dirty little slut," McDermott snarled, his hips thrusting with unyielding determination.

"Ah, fuck, yes!" the stud screamed, their body trembling with overwhelming pleasure.

"That's it, you naughty bitch, give it all to daddy," McDermott commanded, the sound of his balls slapping against the man's ass filling the room.

"God, that was fucking mind-blowing," the slender, youthful stud panted, their hand feverishly working their shaft.

"It sure was," McDermott grinned, his cock pulsating as he released the last surge of cum, sending waves of ecstasy through his body.

$$\Longleftrightarrow$$

"NOW, don't you boys forget the lube," the store owner interjected, a mischievous glint in his eyes. "And let me tell you, those sexy briefs you're wearing, they're on the house if you promise to bless us with another mind-blowing performance."

"Thanks, man, you can count on us coming back for more," the two cops chimed in unison, seizing the bottle of lube as they hastily redressed their electrified bodies.

"Have a damn good time, boys," the owner called after them, his voice dripping with anticipation and desire.

"Oh, believe us, we surely will," the two cops laughed, their senses tingling with the euphoria of their explosive release.

"Shall we hit the road, McDermott?" Fortunato suggested, a seductive hint of mischief in his voice.

"Sounds like the perfect plan," McDermott agreed, his heart pounding with excitement for the untamed adventures ahead, eager to explore every thrilling moment with Fortunato by his side.

CHAPTER 9
"I LOVE YOU, FORTUNATO"

Once they arrived at Fortunato's 3rd-floor walk-up, a sense of unease settled upon the detective. An uncharacteristic silence had replaced McDermott's usually vibrant, bouncy presence, and his avoidance of the older detective raised concerns within Fortunato's mind. Doubts gnawed at him, a fear that he had pushed the younger officer too far, too quickly. The possibility of losing this connection, this burgeoning love, sent a pang of anxiety through Fortunato's heart. He was falling hard and deep for McDermott, unable to deny the intensity of his emotions.

The struggle was real, for McDermott yearned to remain squarely situated in the mold of societal expectations, to be straight in a world that demanded conformity. Fortunato understood the internal conflict tearing at the core of his partner, his stud, but he couldn't deny the authenticity of his own needs and desires. Something was nagging inside him, telling him that McDermott was the man for him. He felt a passion that hadn't stirred within him for far too long. McDermott had awakened something in Fortunato, something he couldn't ignore.

———

FORTUNATO KNEW he wanted this man. He needed him, not just physically but emotionally, in a way that surpassed mere lust. Their shared connection went beyond the physical realm, transcending societal boundaries and expectations. It was a connection that whispered of something deeper, something profound.

Fortunato couldn't help but acknowledge the vulnerability in his own heart. He was willing to fight for this love, navigating the complexities and uncertainties ahead. He knew the risks and challenges they would face, but he couldn't deny the gravity of his feelings. McDermott had become an integral part of his world, and Fortunato was determined to explore the depths of their connection, to embrace the longing that had taken root within him.

Love had found its way into his life, unexpected and powerful. Fortunato couldn't resist its call nor deny the magnetic pull drawing him closer to McDermott. Their journey together would be one of self-discovery, of breaking free from the chains of societal expectations. And as they embarked on this path, Fortunato knew he was ready to face whatever challenges lay ahead, fueled by the undeniable truth that he wanted McDermott with every fiber of his being.

———

DEEP AND RELENTLESS longing had taken root within Fortunato's being. It consumed him, its flames flickering with an intensity he couldn't ignore. It was a yearning that reached far beyond physical desire, transcending the boundaries of mere lust.

In the quiet moments, when his thoughts were his only companion, Fortunato found himself lost in a maze of emotions, a labyrinth of longing that led him straight to McDermott. Images of the younger officer's captivating smile, the way his eyes sparkled with mischief and tenderness, haunted Fortunato's mind, imprinting themselves upon his soul.

The longing pulsed with an ache that resonated deep within his chest. It was a hunger for connection, for a union that surpassed the confines of their professional lives. Fortunato yearned to unravel the layers of McDermott's being, to discover the hidden depths beneath the surface. He craved the intimacy that could only come from baring their souls to one another, exposing the raw vulnerability that resided within.

It was a longing that carried a weight of uncertainty, for Fortunato knew the risks involved. The world could be harsh and unforgiving, and their love dared to challenge its conventions. Yet, despite the potential for heartache and adversity, the yearning within Fortunato remained steadfast and unyielding.

HE DREAMED OF STOLEN MOMENTS, glances, and breaths shared between them. He yearned for the brush of their lips, their bodies' entwining, and their hearts' fusion. The longing burned like a flame, igniting his very existence and driving him to confront his fears and fight for what he believed in.

Fortunato couldn't deny the depth of his feelings, for they were as real as the beating of his heart. McDermott had become more than just a desire; he had become Fortunato's anchor, the missing piece that completed the puzzle of his existence. The longing within him, fierce and unyielding, propelled him forward, urging him to embrace the love that had found its way into his life.

In the face of uncertainty, Fortunato was willing to risk it all. He would face the challenges, navigate the stormy seas, and hold onto the hope that their love would prevail. For in the depths of his being, he knew that McDermott was worth every moment of longing, every ounce of vulnerability, and every step taken on this uncharted path of love.

MCDERMOTT WENT STRAIGHT to the kitchen. A sense of calm settled over him as he poured himself a glass of water. This place, Fortunato's condo, felt like home to the younger cop. But it was more than the physical space—the presence of the older detective, the magnetic pull that drew them together. McDermott had never experienced such a profound connection before. He felt like he was at home when he was with Fortunato. This was something the stud had never felt before.

The realization hit him like a thunderbolt, reverberating through his very soul. Deep in his heart, he had begun to acknowledge the truth—he was gay. And he was ready to accept that part of himself, to embrace it without shame or hesitation. McDermott knew that denying his desires, sexuality, and identity would only lead to a life of emptiness and regret.

Yet, a nagging fear lingered, threatening to overshadow his newfound acceptance. The privilege of being perceived as straight held a weight that McDermott couldn't ignore. He feared the potential loss, judgment, and rejection that might come with openly embracing his true self. The road ahead was uncharted, and uncertainties gnawed at his resolve.

But the clarity washed over him as he stood there, clutching the glass of water in his trembling hand. The truth was undeniable—

he was undeniably, unequivocally gay. And there was one man who had captured his heart, body, and soul—Fortunato.

———

MCDERMOTT'S DESIRE for Fortunato burned with an intensity that couldn't be extinguished. In the depths of his being, he craved the older detective's touch, his closeness, and the connection they shared. It wasn't just physical attraction; it was an all-encompassing need to have Fortunato by his side, to explore the depths of their desires together.

He needed Fortunato like the air he breathed, like a flame seeking fuel. The apprehensions and doubts were no match for the force of his longing. McDermott was ready to step into the uncharted territory of being a proud, out gay man. He was willing to face the challenges and learn how to navigate this new chapter of his life.

The realization was crystal clear, and he couldn't deny it any longer. McDermott wanted Fortunato with every fiber of his being. He craved the passion, intimacy, and love they could share. It was time to cast aside the fears and uncertainties, to embrace his truth, and to pursue the man who had claimed his heart.

———

THE DETERMINATION BLAZED in McDermott's eyes, an unyielding fire that consumed his very being. As his grip on the glass weakened, it slipped from his fingers, crashing into the sink with a resounding shatter. The sound echoed through the room as the glass broke into fragments.

Startled by the noise, Fortunato's instincts kicked in, propelling him from the bedroom to the kitchen instantly. His heart raced, pounding against his chest, as he took in the sight before him.

McDermott, his firm and resilient partner, now leaned over the sink, tears streaming down his face.

Fortunato closed the distance between them without a second thought, his footsteps swift and purposeful. He reached out, his hands gentle yet firm, and pulled McDermott into his embrace. Their bodies collided, a fusion of warmth and strength, as Fortunato enveloped his partner in a cocoon of solace.

McDermott's tears soaked the fabric of Fortunato's shirt as his silent turmoil ravaged his soul. Fortunato held him tight, offering unwavering support and understanding. No words were needed; their connection spoke volumes, transcending the need for verbal reassurance.

As Fortunato held McDermott, he felt the tremors coursing through his partner's body, the weight of their shared journey bearing down upon them both. He knew the path he was internally choosing would be fraught with challenges and uncertainties, but he was determined to weather the storm by McDermott's side.

FORTUNATO WHISPERED WORDS OF COMFORT, his voice a soothing balm against the wounds of doubt and fear. He kissed away the tears that stained McDermott's cheeks, his touch a tender caress that conveyed his unwavering devotion.

They stood there, locked in an embrace, their bodies melded together as they navigated the depths of McDermott's anguish. In that kitchen, surrounded by broken fragments, their love remained unbroken, resilient against the chaos of their emotions.

Slowly, the tears subsided, replaced by a glimmer of hope in McDermott's eyes. He found solace in Fortunato's arms, reassured by the unwavering support that surrounded him. As their breaths intertwined, a silent promise passed between them—a commitment to face the challenges together, to overcome the obstacles that threatened their love, and to emerge stronger on the other side.

MCDERMOTT LOCKED onto Fortunato's eyes, finding protection in their intensity. He felt a surge of emotions pulsed that demanded release. The words tumbled from his lips, raw and unfiltered, coming from the depths of his soul.

"Why are you so fucking perfect?" McDermott's voice quivered with a mix of vulnerability and desire. He needed Fortunato to understand and feel the turmoil that had consumed him for far too long.

Fortunato, attuned to McDermott's unspoken needs, remained silent, allowing him to collect his thoughts and unravel the complex web of emotions that had entangled his heart.

With a deep breath, McDermott summoned all the courage to speak his truth, to lay bare the long-held secret that had weighed upon him. His voice trembled with both fear and the promise of liberation.

"Fortunato, I need you to know that ... I'm gay. There, I said it." McDermott's words carried the weight of a lifetime of denial, of battles fought within the depths of his being. "I know it might come as a surprise, but it's who I am and who I've always been, even when I didn't want to accept it. But now, I can't fight it anymore. The control I thought I had has slipped away. I know it doesn't make sense..."

FORTUNATO'S LIPS PARTED, ready to offer words of understanding and support, but McDermott raised a finger to his mouth, urging him to wait, to listen until he had bared his soul completely.

"Not yet, partner," McDermott implored, his voice trembling. "There's something else I need to say, something that's pretty scary for me because it weighs heavy on my heart. It isn't easy, but I can't keep it hidden any longer. I'm scared, Fortunato. Really scared. Terrified even of losing you." McDermott's voice quivered with the raw intensity of his confession. "But I can't deny it any longer, Fortunato. I love you. I mean, I truly, deeply love you. It's the kind of love that only a man can feel for the one person he longs to be with for eternity. There, I've said it. I love you."

A moment of silence hung heavy in the air, the weight of McDermott's declaration enveloping them both. He braced himself for the possibility of rejection, the shattering of their partnership, and the loss of the connection they had nurtured together.

"OK. Go ahead and say what you need to say. Out with it," McDermott urged. "If this is all too much for you, I can walk away if it's too complicated. Go ahead. Find another partner on the force, one without these complications. I'm ready for whatever comes next, Fortunato. Just speak, dammit."

In that suspended moment, his destiny hung in the balance. McDermott's heart beat with fear and anticipation, his every fiber yearning for Fortunato's response, praying for the affirmation of their love.

———

FORTUNATO'S HEART swelled with tenderness, admiration, and an overwhelming surge of love as he absorbed McDermott's words. The weight of McDermott's vulnerability settled upon him, stirring deep emotions. With a gentle, steady hand, he reached out, cupping McDermott's face, his touch conveying a reassurance that words alone could not express.

"McDermott," Fortunato began, his voice resonating with unwavering devotion, "your truth, your admission—it doesn't scare me in the least. It only strengthens the bond we share. I understand the complexity of your journey and the battles you've had to fight within yourself. And I want you to know that you're not alone in this. I've been by your side, and I always will be. I am so proud to be the first person you came out to. That means the world to me, dude."

Leaning in, Fortunato pressed his lips against McDermott's finger, lingering there momentarily, savoring the taste of their connection, before withdrawing his touch. His eyes, filled with warmth and a profound understanding, met McDermott's gaze with unwavering intensity.

"McDermott, you are so much more than a partner to me," Fortunato whispered, his voice a velvet caress. "You're the missing piece of my soul, the one who has ignited a fire within me I never thought possible. From the moment we met, there was an undeniable pull, a magnetic force drawing us together. And now, with your words, you've laid bare the depths of your heart, revealing a love that resonates with the very core of my being."

⊏══⊐

FORTUNATO'S FINGERS traced a tender path along McDermott's jawline, his touch a delicate reassurance that their connection was unbreakable. "You think this changes things, but it doesn't. It only strengthens the foundation upon which our love is built. McDermott, I love you. Do you hear me? I love you, and I've loved you from the moment we first met, and my love has only grown with each passing day. I want to be the one who holds your hand through the challenges, celebrates your triumphs, and shares a life of passion and devotion with you. I want to be your life partner, not just your partner on the force."

Tears welled in Fortunato's eyes, shimmering with the depth of his emotions. "I don't want to walk away; I want to walk *with* you, side by side, along a path paved with love and understanding. Together, we can navigate the complexities, the doubts, and the fears. We'll build an unshakable future where our love can thrive without boundaries or limitations."

Fortunato's voice, filled with a tender resolve, resonated with an unwavering promise. "So, McDermott, my love, I'm not rejecting you. I'm embracing you. I'm embracing us. Let our hearts intertwine, and let our love be a beacon of strength and acceptance. I choose you, now and forever. So, dude, I'm not gonna let you go."

Time seemed to stand still in that suspended moment, their hearts attuned to the symphony of love that echoed between them. McDermott's fears melted away, replaced by a profound sense of belonging, as they embarked on a shared journey, united by a love that knew no bounds.

<hr />

AS THEIR DESIRE SURGED, they instinctively headed toward the bedroom. With hunger, they shed their clothes, the air crackling with anticipation. Each touch, each graze of skin against skin, fueled the fire that burned within them.

Lips locked in a passionate embrace, they stumbled toward the bed, their bodies entwined in a dance of need and longing. The soft fabric of the sheets welcomed them, a sanctuary for their passions to unfold.

Exploring hands roamed hungrily, tracing the contours of sculpted bodies with genuine desire. They reveled in the power of touch, the electric sparks that ignited their senses. Every caress and stroke sent shivers of pleasure cascading through their veins.

Their mouths sought out one another, tongues colliding in a dance of shared ecstasy. Moans mingled and filled the room as they lost themselves in the intoxicating taste of desire. No words were needed; their bodies spoke a language of longing and pleasure that only they understood.

Tonight would be no different than future nights. They came in each other's arms, shooting a release onto each other that would bond them for the night.

$$\rule{0.8cm}{0.3em}$$

TO BE CONTINUED...

This book is dedicated to all the dreamers who, like myself, spent their youth wandering the streets of Boston in their imaginations, captivated by crime detection. We yearned for a place where we could rest our weary legs on the back of cop cars, where we could seek out partners amidst the hallowed halls of police locker rooms, and where we could find a male character who would ignite passionate nights within the corridors of stakeouts in abandoned warehouses. Ah, the irresistible allure of the charismatic Detective Lance Fortunato and the world he inhabits has captured our hearts and fired our imaginations.

To my dear readers, I extend my heartfelt gratitude for allowing me to accompany you on this thrilling journey as an author. I still remember my youthful days, a mere high school student at the tender age of 18, when I, too, yearned for my very own Detective Fortunato to sweep me off my feet and join me in the exhilarating adventures life had in store. The memories of those times, filled with hope and dreams, hold a special place in my heart.

With the utmost gratitude and respect, I present this work to you. It is a humble offering, a tale woven with passion and love, inspired by a vision of a world where love knows no boundaries and where the captivating atmosphere of police precincts serves as a backdrop for our most cherished desires.

May this book serve as a conduit, transporting you to a realm where dreams come alive, love reigns supreme, and the essence of intense gay passion between men takes center stage.

With deep gratitude and respect,

Griff Holland

ABOUT THE AUTHOR

Griff Holland is a remarkable individual who defies the notion of an ordinary author. By day, he showcases his exceptional skills as a master architect, renowned for his expertise in preserving and revitalizing New England's historic treasures. With an artist's touch, he breathes new life into cherished landmarks, leaving a lasting impact on the architectural world. However, Griff's talents extend far beyond his architectural prowess.

In his earlier days, Griff was an Olympic skier, an adventurer who reveled in the thrill of pushing himself to the limits. The snow-covered peaks became his playground, and the adrenaline rush left an indelible mark on his soul. It is this exhilaration that spills onto the pages of his male erotica fiction, infusing his stories with a sense of passion and excitement.

When Griff is not immersed in the world of architectural restoration or embracing the thrill of alpine adventures, he seeks solace and purpose at his writing desk. Within the sanctuary of his imagination, he weaves intricate tales of male desire that transcend the ordinary. His plots are captivating, and his characters are complex, ensnaring readers from the very first sentence until the final page.

Yet, Griff's talents do not stop there. He is also a sought-after public speaker, frequently gracing television screens as an expert on home repair. He shares his knowledge and expertise with a warmth and approachability that endears him to all who encounter him, inspiring and motivating others along the way. His enthusiasm is contagious, making him a cherished figure in the literary world.

In the precious moments of free time, he cherishes, Griff embarks on outdoor escapades with his beloved canine companions. A devoted dog lover, he finds solace in nature's embrace, which rejuvenates his spirit and fuels his creativity.

Despite the accolades he has received, Griff remains remarkably humble and grounded. He is an eternal student of his craft, constantly seeking improvement and growth. Whether conquering snow-capped peaks or putting pen to paper, he approaches each endeavor with unwavering determination and an unwavering commitment to excellence.

Thus, the enigmatic and multifaceted Griff Holland continues to leave an indelible mark on the world. He is an artist of architecture, an adventurer of the slopes, a captivating author of desire, and a beacon of inspiration for all those who yearn to embrace their passions and forge their paths.

ACKNOWLEDGMENTS

First and foremost, the author extends heartfelt gratitude to the dedicated gay erotica enthusiasts whose passion and enthusiasm form the foundation of the stories in this collection. It is important to note that these tales are presented as works of fiction, aiming to celebrate the wide range of human desire and sensuality that knows no boundaries. The men within these pages are courageous and unapologetically themselves, finding strength in embracing their sexuality and sensuality. They forge connections and camaraderie with fellow individuals who appreciate thoughtfully crafted erotica. The daring spirits of these readers, the kinksters, inspire and breathe life into these stories, allowing them to unfold and thrive.

The author expresses deep gratitude to their beloved partner, Mitchell, whose unwavering support has been invaluable. Mitchell's love and encouragement have been the guiding light that led the author to bring this book to fruition. In the quiet moments at home, their presence is enchanting. Mitchell's constant inspiration extends even to the gym, where they make the author feel like the best version of themselves. The author is grateful for the solid foundation Mitchell has provided for this creative journey.

Appreciation is sincerely extended to the editor and beta readers for their invaluable feedback and guidance. Their keen insights and thoughtful suggestions have shaped the story into its final form. Their unwavering commitment to excellence has been instrumental in the creation of this work. The author deeply cherishes their attention to detail and dedication to refining the story.

A special tribute is dedicated to the LGBTQ+ community, whose tireless advocacy and unwavering fight for equality and acceptance have paved the way for stories like this to be told and embraced. The community's resilience in the face of adversity serves as a beacon of hope and inspiration. The author stands in awe of their continued activism, which has brought about significant change throughout history.

The author extends heartfelt gratitude to the dear readers for embarking on this journey together. He sincerely hopes this collection of stories has brought joy, pleasure, and a deeper appreciation for the complexities of love, desire, and human connection. The readers' support has been the driving force behind the author's creativity, and their willingness to explore this world alongside him fills his heart with profound gratitude.

May these tales of passion and romance continue to resonate in the readers' hearts, celebrating the beauty of love in all its forms. The author thanks each and every reader for being an integral part of this creative adventure. They hope storytelling's power will inspire and unite everyone who encounters these pages.

READERS—GOT IDEAS?

Griff Holland, an author whose talents shine in the realm of erotica, finds himself entangled in an intriguing predicament. The abundance of creativity from his devoted readers is both a blessing and a challenge. Their ceaseless stream of story ideas is a testament to his magnetic storytelling, but it also takes its toll on his muse, leaving her in dire need of respite.

As the morning sun casts its gentle glow upon his writing chamber, Griff opens his email inbox to discover a veritable flood of tantalizing story ideas from his ardent admirers. With eager anticipation, he delves into each missive, immersing himself in the sea of imagination that lies before him. The outpouring of passion and ingenuity within those emails is nothing short of astounding. Some readers pen comprehensive plotlines with vivid character descriptions that breathe life into their envisioned worlds. Others choose a more abstract approach, crafting mere fragments of scenes or intriguing situations that capture their imagination.

Griff is humbled by the trust bestowed upon him by his readers. Their unwavering faith in his storytelling prowess is a privilege and a responsibility he holds dear. Determined to honor their dedication and the exuberance they bring to his craft, he resolves to create an announcement that will further fuel their creativity.

Seated at his writing desk, Griff pens a carefully worded missive, inviting his audience to join him in weaving tales that push the boundaries of imagination. He encourages them to unleash their wildest notions, assuring them that no concept will be deemed too audacious. After all, his enduring mantra has always been, "No kink is too kinky."

Griff feels a flutter of excitement in his heart with the announcement destined to grace his website and adorn the pages of his upcoming books and stories. His readers are an integral part of his creative journey, and he knows that their collaboration will elevate his work to heights he can scarcely conceive. As the ink dries on his announcement, he sends it forth into the digital world, eagerly awaiting the responses that will soon fill his inbox. Griff yearns to unravel the enigma of their collective imaginations and the stories that will emerge from the amalgamation of their dreams and his craft.

In the following days, the flood of ideas surges again, and Griff finds himself immersed in a treasure trove of inspiration. Each email contains a universe of passion and desire, waiting to be crafted into compelling narratives that delight his readers.

With boundless enthusiasm, he delves into the task at hand, weaving together the threads of his readers' ideas with his inimitable style. The result is a collection of tales that span the spectrum of human desires, transporting readers to familiar and unexplored realms.

Griff and his readers form an unbreakable bond through their shared creativity, a communion of hearts and minds united by the power of storytelling. The journey ahead promises adventure, passion, and revelations, and together, they venture forth into the uncharted territories of the human imagination, leaving a trail of tantalizing tales in their wake.

To contribute story ideas, readers are invited to email Griff at: Griff.Holland.Writer@gmail.com

Printed in Dunstable, United Kingdom